Just add water!

# Sequins for Sea Queens

Read other titles in the series

1 No Ordinary Girl

2 Living With Secrets

3 Fishy Business

4 A Sleepover Tail

# Sequins for Sea Queens

Adapted by Sue Behrent



SIMON AND SCHUSTER

**SIMON AND SCHUSTER**
First published in Great Britain in 2010 by Simon & Schuster UK Ltd,
1st Floor, 222 Gray's Inn Road, London WC1X 8HB
A CBS Company
Originally published in Australia in 2007 by Parragon
Licenced by ZDF Enterprises GmbH, Mainz


A CIP catalogue record for this book is available from the British Library

ISBN 978-1-84738-541-3

10 9 8 7 6 5 4 3 2 1

Printed by CPI Cox & Wyman, Reading, Berkshire RG1 8EX

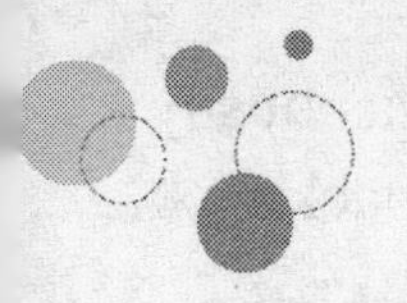

# Chapter 1

The waves rolled gently onto the beach as Lewis and Emma pulled their boat away from the shoreline, closer to the ring of trees that lined the island. It was a beautiful sunny day with only a very light breeze blowing, *perfect conditions for conducting some serious investigations*, thought Lewis as he looked about.

"So, *this* is the place that turned you into a fish?" he asked in a matter-of-fact tone.

"A *mermaid*, Lewis," replied Emma, rolling her eyes.

"Yeah, that's what I meant," said Lewis distractedly as he turned and gazed up at the huge bare mountain-rock that jutted up out of the middle of the island. With a little imagination he could see how it might look like a shark jumping up out of the water and supposed that was how the place got its name: Mako Island.

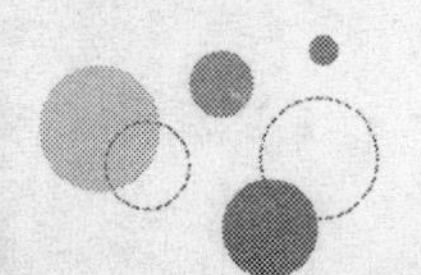



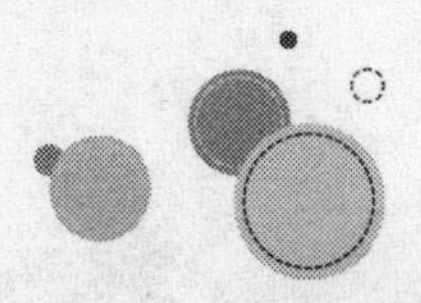

ooked back at Emma who was busily
he gear they'd need into her backpack.

on't know, I just expected something a
more… Club Med," he said, trying not to sound too disappointed. *Or at least a bit more dramatic or scary*, he thought to himself. But he wouldn't dare say something like that to Emma. She'd only roll her eyes and scoff at him. As it was, Emma raised her eyebrows haughtily and stalked up the beach. *She's definitely the level-headed one of the three*, Lewis thought as he hastily grabbed his equipment and ran after Emma as she disappeared into the dense forest.

They walked for some time through the thick forest. The trees were so close together that the sun's rays had difficulty penetrating the canopy of leaves above, giving everything at ground level a dark, mysterious look. It was cool in the shade, but after carrying a tripod and various other bits of complicated equipment for forty-five minutes or so, Lewis was starting to sweat. And he was a mozzie magnet! He must've been bitten six or seven times already!

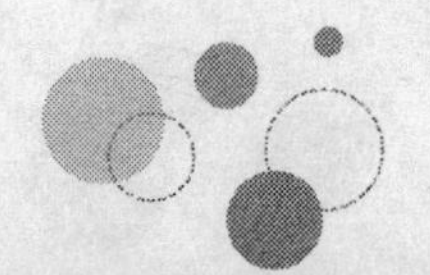

He stopped for breath and rummaged around in his bag for his drink bottle. Emma, still as cool and fresh as when they'd started out, went on a few steps and then sensing that Lewis had stopped, turned around to see if he was okay. *Poor Lewis* – she thought to herself as she watched him, red faced and tired, slapping away yet another mosquito – *he's not used to such physical exercise.* But Lewis was smart – *really* smart – and Emma believed if anyone could find out why they'd turned into mermaids out here on Mako Island, then Lewis was their guy. Even though she, Rikki and Cleo had tried to keep their mermaidness a secret from everyone, she was glad in some ways that Lewis had discovered their secret that day at Miriam's pool party. It was a relief to Emma to just be able to relax around someone and not be on her guard all the time in case she accidentally got splashed with water! Her swimming trial days seemed very long ago…

Emma shook her shoulders and came back to herself with a start.

Lewis was glugging water from a bottle and

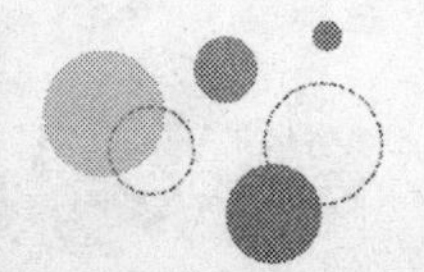



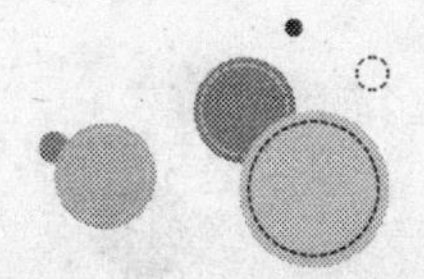

scratching his leg where a particularly nasty mozzie bite was starting to come up.

"See that volcano?" said Emma, pointing to it looming in the distance. "The caves are up there."

"*What*? Way up there?" Lewis spluttered, staring past Emma's outstretched arm.

They looked at each other. Emma arched her eyebrows again, daring Lewis to complain about the distance they had yet to travel.

"I want to find out how this happened," she said. "And that takes hard work, Lewis. Come on!"

She grabbed the tripod off the ground, slung it over her shoulder and trudged on. Lewis wanted to tell her he could carry all the equipment, but he didn't. Mostly because he knew he couldn't!

They heard the rushing river for a long time before they saw it. In the quiet of the forest, it had sounded like a huge great torrent and when they finally came to the clearing, Lewis

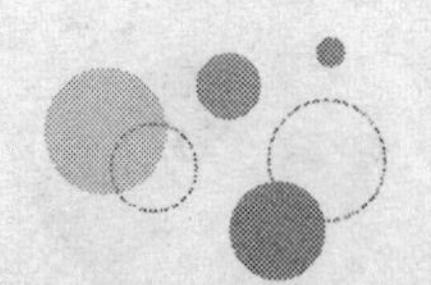



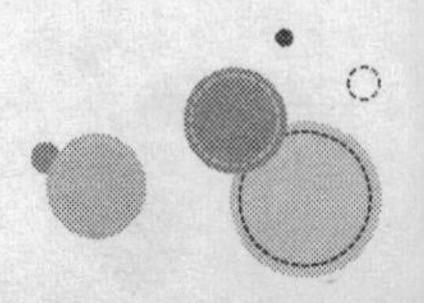

was surprised to see that it was neither as wide nor as strong as he'd imagined. It *was* a beautiful spot though. *There must be a natural underground spring here somewhere*, he thought as he watched the cool dark water flow around the large boulders that stood in the middle of the river.

Emma had scrambled up on top of one of the largest of the boulders and was pointing away from where Lewis was standing on the bank.

"The entrance is down there near the waterfall," yelled Emma above the din of the water. "I can't get any closer or I'll..."

"I know, the whole beached whale thing," Lewis called back.

"*Mermaid*, Lewis!" said Emma, huffily. Lewis snickered to himself; Emma really was fun to tease!

"Yes, that is what I meant," he said, straight-faced, as he passed Emma his bag and the rest of the equipment he was carrying and jumped across to join her on top of the boulder.

He looked down over the edge to where

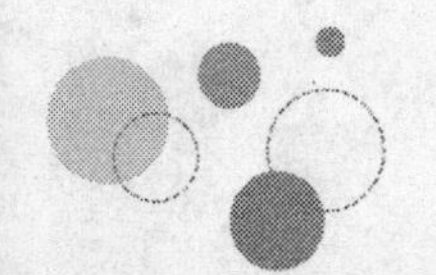



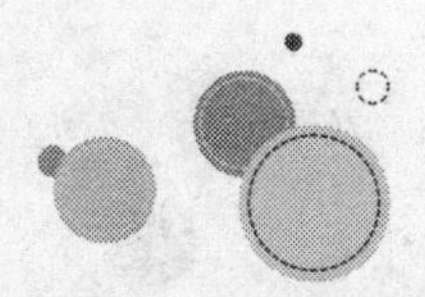

Emma had pointed, but couldn't see any cave entrance.

"So, how do *you* get in?" he asked.

"Swim," replied Emma, matter-of-factly. "There's an underwater entrance."

"Swim?" said Lewis, angrily. "So the hike was optional? I could have *swum*?" He swatted a passing fly with annoyance.

"Fifty metres, without coming up for air," said Emma, mechanically.

"Right, point taken, air is good," said Lewis, somewhat mollified. "Anyway, it's better that I discover the pool the same way you did. It's much more scientific that way." He nodded his head a couple of times. *Yes, much more scientific… and far less of a hazard to my health*, he thought.

Lewis peered over the side again, but he still couldn't be sure of where the entrance was and he wasn't about to ask Emma – she already thought he was halfway to useless.

"Just be careful you don't fall…" said

Emma, handing Lewis her stuff. She couldn't swim with her backpack; Lewis was going to have to take her gear with him.

"Oh Emma, *please*. I *am* a scientist," said Lewis, confidently. "And I know *exactly* what I'm doing… ahhhhhh."

And with that, Lewis lost his footing and tumbled down into the cave, just like the three girls had before him all those weeks ago.

Emma laughed out loud. *Really, Lewis can be ridiculously pompous sometimes*, she thought to herself, then quickly felt bad about laughing at him. After all, he *was* helping them.

"I'll meet you down there!" she yelled guiltily.

But if someone had been around to see Emma skip lightly to the river bank and re-enter the forest, they would have also heard her hoot with laughter as she remembered the look on Lewis's face immediately after he lost his balance!

"*Wow*," exclaimed Lewis softly, peering into

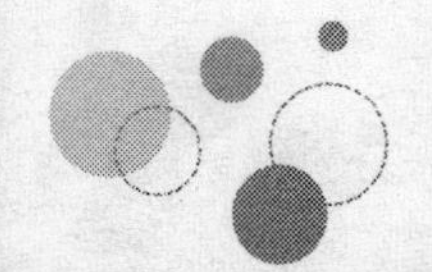



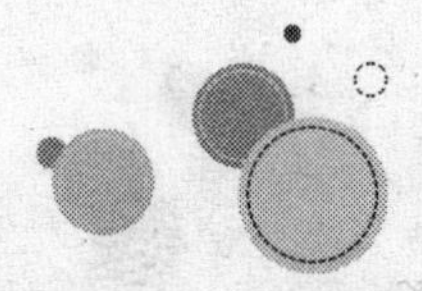

the gloom of the cave and up through the hole in the ceiling to the sunny blue sky beyond.

*We're obviously standing in a massive extinct volcano*, he thought wonderingly, *I bet hundreds of people from lost civilizations have stood here before us worshipping their gods. This place is awesome!* Lewis was sure they'd come to the right place. If they were going to find the answer to the mystery of why the girls had become mermaids, they'd find it here.

"Pretty cool, huh?" said Emma matter-of-factly. She stood looking at him searchingly for a minute with her hands on her hips, but when Lewis still hadn't made a move to unpack the gear, Emma began to tap her foot impatiently.

"Uh, so, where do we start?" she asked edgily.

Lewis snapped out of his dream and instantly became all business-like, pacing around the small cave as he spoke.

"First I'd like to map the space, and then get some rock and some water samples for testing. Something in this environment triggered your transformation." He paused to

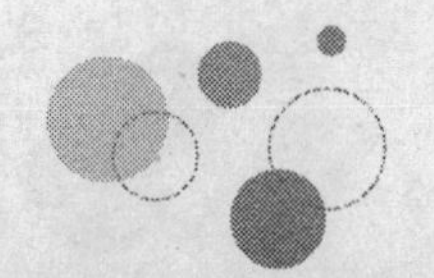



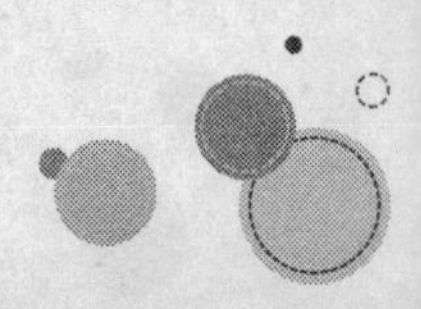

examine something on the cave floor. "And if I can figure out what that something was," he straightened up and smiled at Emma, "I can figure out how you got your tail… and *then* start asking why."

Emma smiled at him. *He may be a flake, but he's* our *flake and knows what he's doing*, she thought happily. Emma was confident Lewis would come through for them.

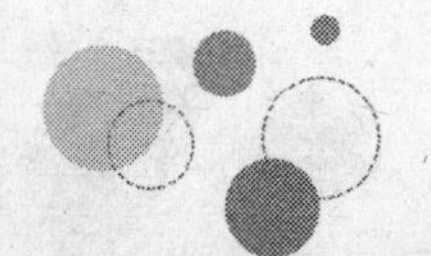



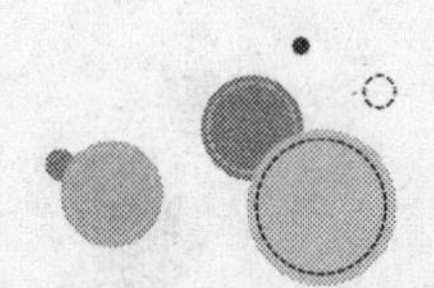

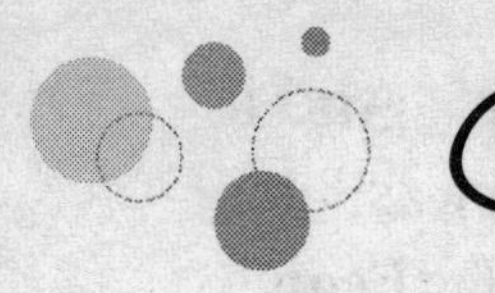

# Chapter 2

Rikki had already ordered a banana smoothie and was seated at one of the banks of internet terminals when Cleo walked in. The Juice-Net Café was one of Cleo's favourite hangouts and Rikki had parked herself there knowing that sooner or later Cleo would turn up. Cleo smiled, gave her a little wave and went and sat down in a booth to wait until Rikki had finished using the internet.

Cleo flicked through a magazine while she waited, but growing quickly bored of that, she settled on watching Rikki work.

*She sure has a lot of things to write to people about*, thought Cleo idly as she watched Rikki, head down, furiously tapping on the keyboard. *I wish that I had an interesting life to write about. Oh, I mean I wish I had an interesting life I could* tell *people about! Instead I have to keep all the mermaid stuff such a big secret between me and my diary. Like, who would believe me*

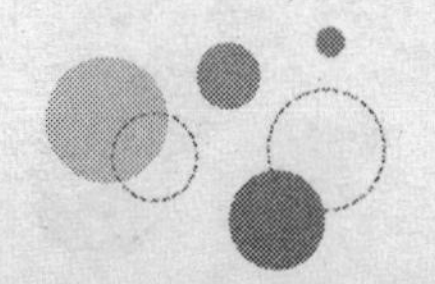



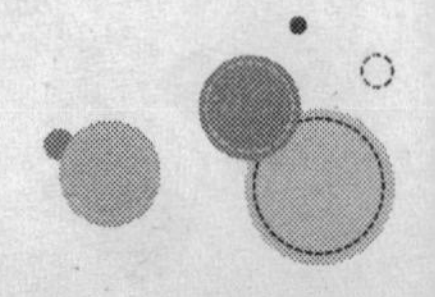

*if I* did *accidentally tell someone!* She sighed deeply. *This kind of negative attitude will get me nowhere*, she thought, trying to distract herself. She looked over at Rikki again. *Rikki would look* sooo *great if she'd wear a bit more colour*, Cleo thought, *all those blacks and khakis… she should wear something in a lighter shade.*

"I'm just finishing up here – won't be a second," Rikki called across the room to Cleo. She'd been busy writing a video game review for an online magazine, when she'd become aware of the feeling of someone's eyes boring into the back of her head. And when she'd turned around, Cleo had been staring absently at her. *Sometimes she seems like she's in another world!* thought Rikki.

"Is there something wrong?" she asked with a puzzled look.

Cleo blushed hotly. She hadn't meant to stare at Rikki and now she felt embarrassed that she'd been caught out.

"Nothing, Rikki. I was just thinking about something," said Cleo, smiling weakly.

Rikki smiled back and went on with what

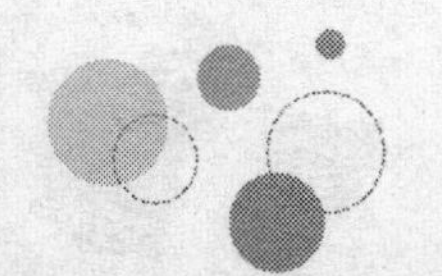



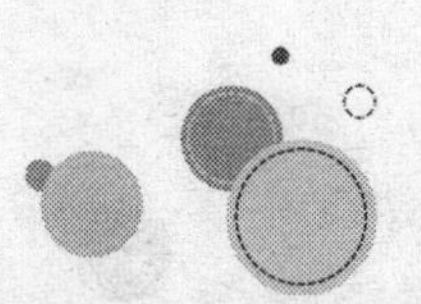

she was doing.

Cleo sighed again before getting up and going over to the counter to order a juice. While she waited she noticed some leaflets advertising upcoming events at the Juice-Net Café; there was a trivia night on Tuesday, but Cleo didn't think she was smart enough for that. Emma, on the other hand, would be great at trivia. *I must remember to tell her about it*, thought Cleo. *Oh, there's a* Clean Up The Beach Rally *next week. I wonder if that's the thing Emma's been talking about... hey, what's this?* Cleo spied a handout for something called 'The Miss Sea Queen Pageant'. It looked like some kind of beauty contest, except that instead of bikinis and ball gowns, the pictures made it look like it was all about who came in the best sea-themed costume. Plus, it was on at the marine park where Cleo worked. *Why haven't I heard of this?* she thought excitedly. She grabbed the pamphlet and took her drink back to the table.

'Could you be the next *Miss Sea Queen*?

Find out by registering at the marine park by Sunday 14th and come and join the fun! Entry: **free**.'

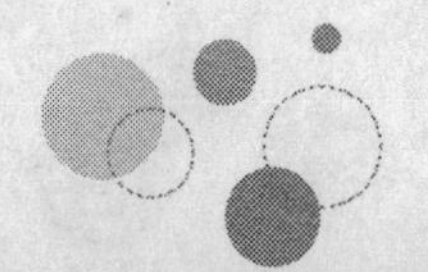



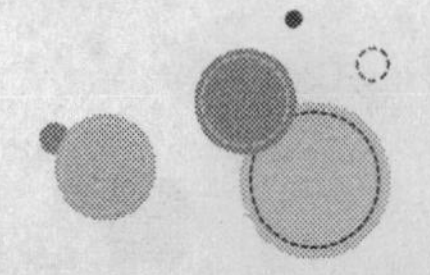

Cleo's mind went into overdrive. *A beauty pageant! How exciting!* she thought happily; *Imagine if I won! I wonder what the prizes are... not that it matters of course*, she added hurriedly to herself. It was the entering that counted, naturally.

Cleo felt the jolt of someone sitting down in the booth opposite her. She peeped over the top of the flyer she was holding and saw Rikki smiling faintly at her, twirling her straw around her now empty glass.

"You look all bright-eyed and bushy tailed!" said Rikki. "What's got you looking so pleased with yourself?" Rikki held out her hand for the flyer.

Reluctantly, Cleo handed it across.

"The Miss Sea Queen Pageant!?" said Rikki, disgustedly. "How sexist can you get? What kind of a *moron* would enter something like this?!"

Cleo smiled tightly. It was pretty much the exact reaction she'd have expected from Rikki. *Really it's none of her business what type of moron... no wait, I don't mean* moron, *I'm not a moron...*

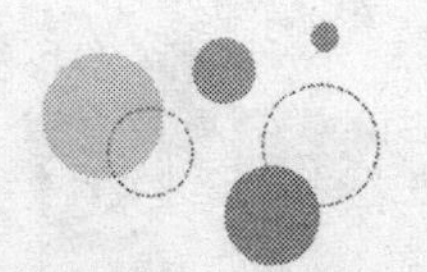



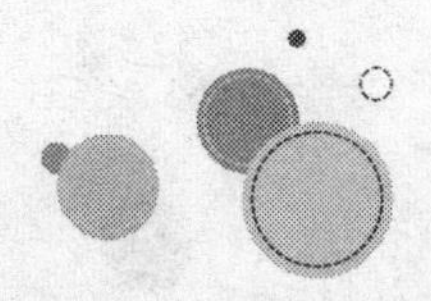

But before Cleo could get her confused thoughts in order, she was distracted by the sound of the door to the Juice-Net Café banging open and closed, followed by the sound of Miriam's voice carrying loudly over the conversations of the kids already in the café.

"… and I said to him, like, no *way* would I be seen dead with *you*. And you know what he said?" Miriam asked.

Miriam's best friend Tiffany shook her head, hanging on Miriam's every word.

"He said… wait for this… *he* said 'But if you didn't want to go out with me, why did you agree to come down to the beach?' and I said 'Because I'd never ridden on the back of a motorbike before!' Can you believe he thought I was *into* him?" Miriam and Tiffany laughed loudly, all the while looking around the café to see if there was anyone cool they might want to hang out with.

Miriam spotted Cleo and smiled at Tiffany, flicking her eyes over in Cleo and Rikki's direction – *Let's have some fun*, Miriam seemed to be saying. It's wasn't that Miriam

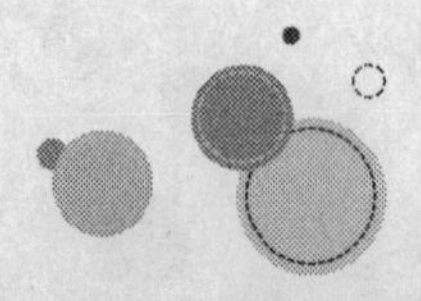

disliked Cleo exactly, but it annoyed Miriam to be around someone that sweet. Plus she'd never got to the bottom of that mystery at her pool party and still laid the blame squarely on Cleo's shoulders. Everything had been going okay at that party before Cleo's friend Lewis had arrived, complete with fishing gear, and disappeared out the back. Then the sliding door had somehow locked itself and when they'd finally managed to get it open and free themselves from the kitchen, the pool water had gone. *Literally disappeared*. Miriam didn't know how they'd done it, but she knew that Cleo and Lewis were behind it, somehow.

Miriam and Tiffany wandered over towards the booth and saw the flyer Rikki had dropped on the table in front of her.

Miriam looked at Rikki in pretend-shock.

"*You're* not thinking of entering the Miss Sea Queen Pageant are you?" she asked with an obvious sneer in her voice.

"I'd rather drop *dead*," Rikki replied angrily.

*The only way to handle Miriam is to ignore her*, thought Rikki, annoyed at herself for

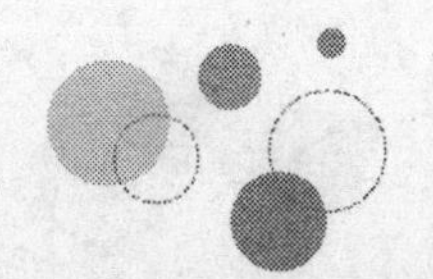



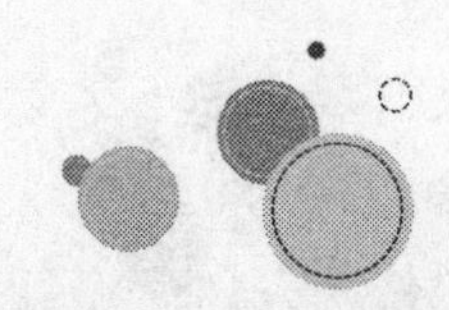

being angry at all. *And now I've given her the satisfaction of answering her*, she thought irritably. But Rikki couldn't have *anyone* thinking that she'd be lame enough to enter a pathetic beauty pageant!

Miriam looked at her with mock-pity. It was a convincing look, because Miriam practised it in the mirror in the mornings when she brushed her teeth.

"It's just that *I'm* entering,"she went on.

Cleo moved restlessly in her seat and looked as if she was about to say something. That was all that Miriam needed.

"Oh... if *you're* thinking of entering, Cleo, a word of advice. *Don't bother*," she said.

"That's *two* words," Rikki scoffed, before saying the word *idiot* under her breath. She hated to hear Cleo talked down to and Miriam was so good at it.

"*And* Cleo wouldn't be interested in prancing across a stage wearing a clingy dress," added Rikki.

Miriam hissed out a breath and stared

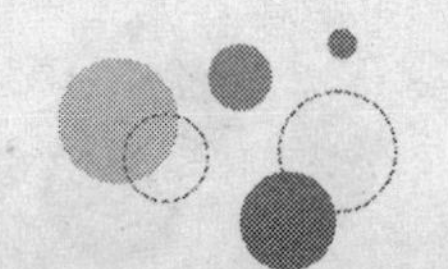

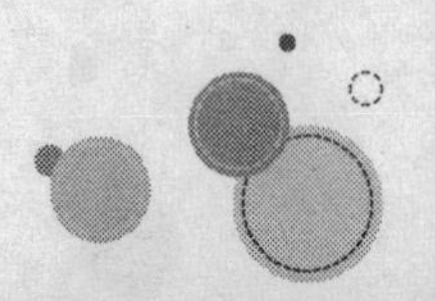

moodily at her.

"It's a costume, *actually*," said Miriam, pulling a face.

"With a sea motif," chimed in Tiffany.

Miriam struck a pose. "I've *always* had an affinity with the sea..." said Miriam, dreamily running her hands through her long, beautiful hair.

Cleo, who had been listening patiently to Miriam and Rikki, felt her self-control snap. She didn't care if Miriam was going to compete in the contest or if Rikki thought it was sexist rubbish, she was going to enter and win the Miss Sea Queen Pageant and she didn't mind one bit what people thought of her.

But Miriam's empty boast about her one-with-sea-ness! *As if!!* Cleo thought wildly.

"*You*? That's a joke." Cleo said angrily. "*I'm* the one with the affinity! I'm a..."

Rikki had a feeling she knew what was coming next and gave Cleo a quick kick under the table to shut her up.

The last thing they needed was Cleo blurting

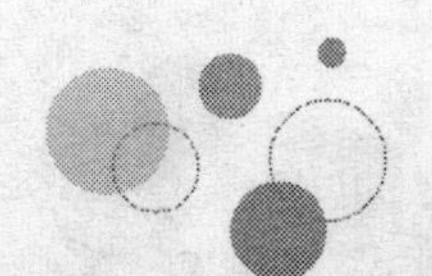



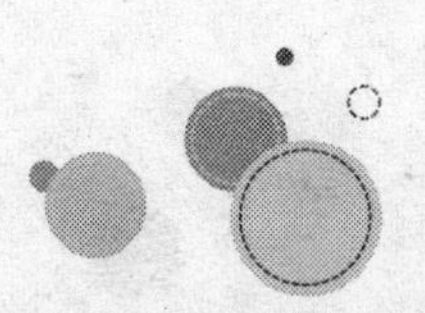

out that she was a mermaid!

But Miriam was already bored with the conversation and wasn't paying any attention to Cleo's little temper tantrum.

"Let's go, Tiffany. I have to pick up a few more accessories for my costume," she said. And with a final smirk and a flick of her hair, Miriam was gone.

Rikki leaned across the table.

"What was all that about?" she asked Cleo in a low voice.

"What do you mean?" Cleo replied.

"You know what. You were just going to say you were a mermaid," Rikki whispered back. "We have to be more careful."

Cleo groaned. "I know, I'm sorry. It's just that Miriam makes me *so* mad sometimes. I'll be careful, Rikki, I promise."

Rikki chewed her straw thoughtfully and looked at Cleo. "Yeah, well make sure you are."

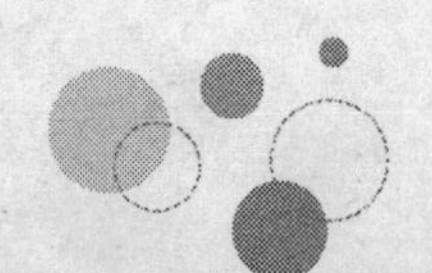



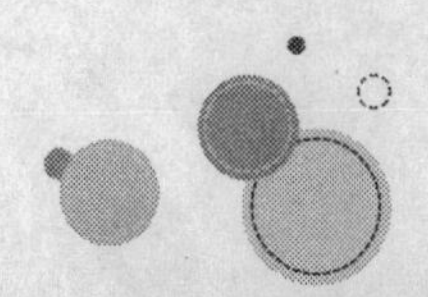

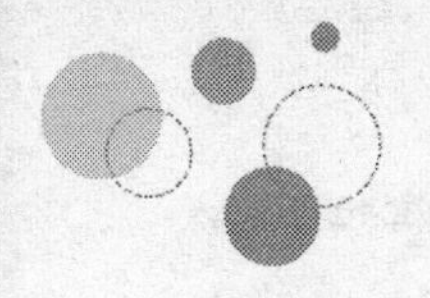

# Chapter 3

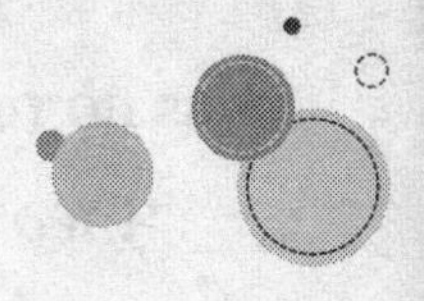

Cleo's little sister Kim was in her bedroom getting ready to meet some friends down at the Juice-Net Café. She was thinking carefully about her outfit, because she figured there might be some boys down there; you just never know!

She held up a skirt in front of herself and checked out the look in the mirror.

*I look like I'm trying too hard*, she thought, throwing the skirt onto an ever-growing pile of clothes on her bed.

She rummaged around in her closet for a pair of patched jeans and held them up for inspection.

*Perfect! Now I just need a belt... oh, Cleo has a belt that would look brilliant with these jeans*, she thought happily.

She opened her bedroom door.

"Cleo?" she called down the hallway. There

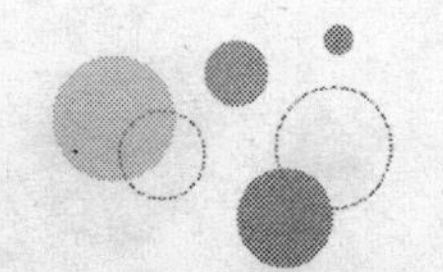



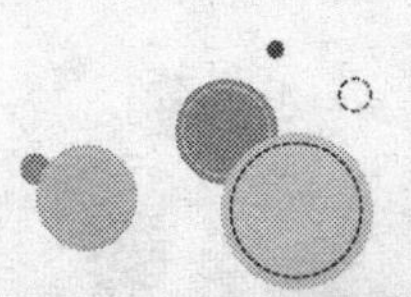

was no reply from Cleo's room.

"*Cleo*?!" Kim called again with impatience.

Downstairs she could hear her mum vacuuming. If Cleo was downstairs she'd never hear Kim calling for her over the noise of the vacuum.

Kim sighed theatrically and flounced down the hall to the top of the stairs.

"*Cleo*?!" she called again.

Downstairs, Cleo's mum shut off the vacuum. She thought she could hear someone yelling.

"*Cleooooooooo*?!" shouted Kim again from the top of the stairs.

In the now quiet house, Kim's voice echoed loudly.

Mrs Sertori went to the bottom of the stairs and looked up quizzically at her youngest daughter.

"Oh, Mum," said Kim, the volume of her voice dropping back to normal. "Have you seen Cleo?"

"I think she went out," replied Mrs Sertori.

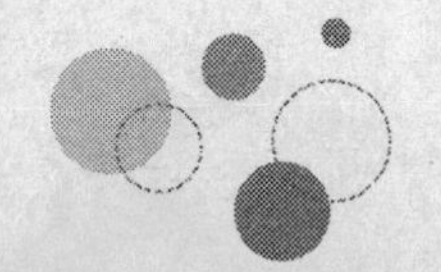



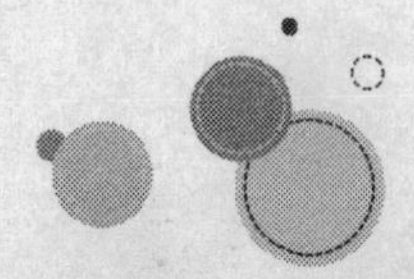

Kim stuck out her bottom lip in a pout.

"She's *never* here any more," she said sulkily.

Mrs Sertori felt sorry for Kim. She knew it was difficult for Kim being on her own a lot of the time, when she'd really have liked to be hanging out with her older, cooler sister.

"I'm sure she'll make time for you if you want to play with her," said her mum encouragingly.

Kim rolled her eyes and sneered at her mother.

"*Play* with her?" said Kim with disbelief. "*No way*! I just wanted to borrow her belt!"

*Sometimes Mum has no idea*! thought Kim as she stomped down the hall. *As if I'd want to* play *with Cleo! Lame!*

Her mother shrugged her shoulders; she didn't know what had gotten into Kim lately.

Upstairs, Kim stayed in her room until she heard her mum restart the vacuum cleaner and then quietly opened her bedroom door and

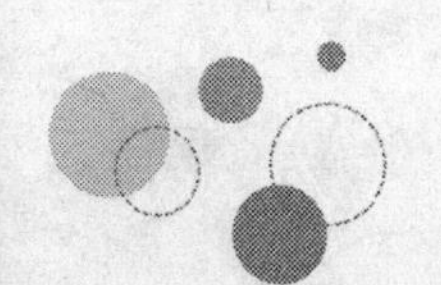



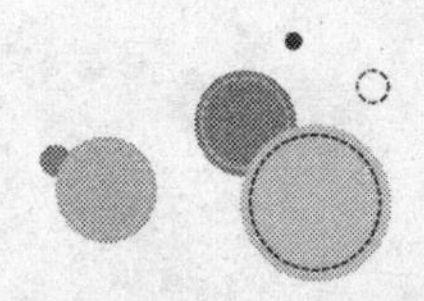

snuck down the hallway into Cleo's room.

Cleo was well known for being the tidiest person in the family and her bedroom was a great example of that reputation! Everything was spotless and in its place, her homework stacked neatly on the desk and her fishbowl sparkling in the sunlight. *She's always cleaning that fishbowl*, Kim thought to herself distractedly, looking about to see where Cleo might keep her belts. *This is going to be easy*.

She made her way over to the wardrobe first and flung open the door.

CRASH!

A heap of books and sports equipment came tumbling out. Kim winced. She hoped her mother hadn't heard the noise. She stood and listened for a minute, but the drone of the vacuum cleaner continued. *So*, she thought, *this is how she keeps everything so tidy. She just stuffs it all in here*. She looked at the mess of the wardrobe and shook her head, thinking that perhaps it wasn't going to be so easy to find the belt after all.

Kim reached into the back of the wardrobe

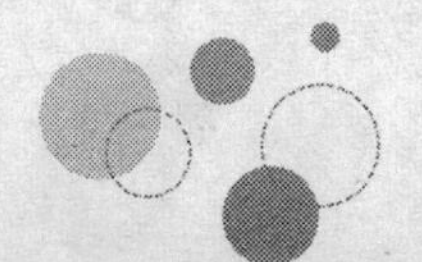



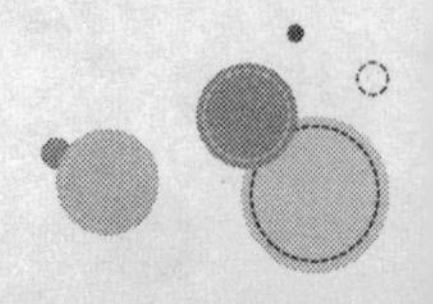

to see if there were any belts slung over the coat hooks, but there was nothing there. She pulled back a couple of hangers; nothing.

*I'm going to be here all day!* thought Kim, desperately checking her watch. She was meeting the girls from school in 45 minutes. *I need to think. Where do I keep* my *belts?*

She raced over to the dresser, opened the top drawer and started rifling through Cleo's things.

*T-shirt, t-shirt, t-shirt... oh, what's this?*

Kim pulled a book out from under the pile of t-shirts.

"My secret life…" she read aloud.

*This could be interesting*, Kim thought excitedly as she flicked through the pages of drawings.

There were sketches of what looked like Cleo and her friends Rikki and Emma, but there was something strange about them. In every picture, their legs were drawn weirdly. In fact, it almost looked like Cleo had drawn them with fish tails instead of legs. Kim was

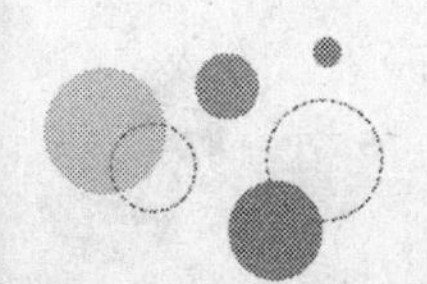



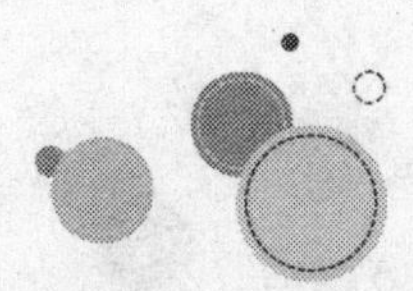

well aware that Cleo wasn't exactly the most artistically gifted member of their family, but even so, she knew that there was something not quite right about these drawings. There were also several pages with sketches of a menacing-looking island as well as diagrams of cave networks and rock pools.

All the writing was in some sort of secret language that Kim couldn't work out.

"This is weird," she said, frustrated. It might take some time to work out the key to the code, but Kim was smart and she knew if it took all day, she'd be able to discover the clues she needed. *My dear sister just isn't that clever*, she thought to herself and smiled.

She stuffed the diary under her shirt and quickly left the room, closing the door on her way out.

The belt was the furthest thing from her mind.

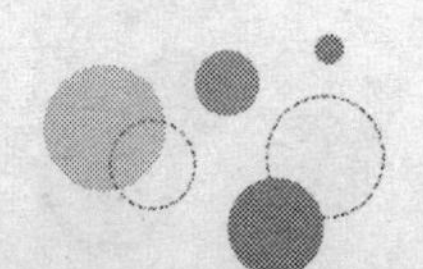



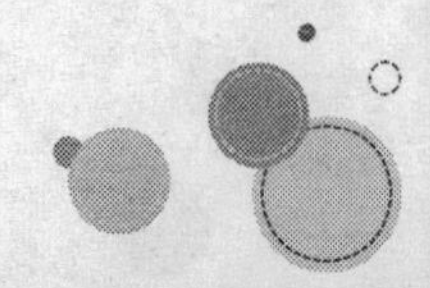

Cleo smiled pleasantly.

"Flavours?" she asked.

"You choose. I'm feeling… spontaneous," Miriam replied, flicking her hair off her shoulder and looking around as if to see if anyone was watching her. "And *ultra* confident. I've finished the preparations for the competition." She watched Cleo closely to see if this little piece of information annoyed her. "I have a costume that's to *die* for."

"To *die* for," chimed in Tiffany.

Cleo, head down, rummaged around in the mini freezer for the ice-creams.

*If only I had a horrible flavour to give her*, Cleo thought, irritated by Miriam's ability to get under her skin. She wondered how Tiffany could put up with her constant bragging! *If only there was a potato and leek flavoured ice-cream or something. I bet Lewis could invent that!*

Instead all she could find was a raspberry and lemon gelato, which she offered them.

Miriam took hers with a half smile and

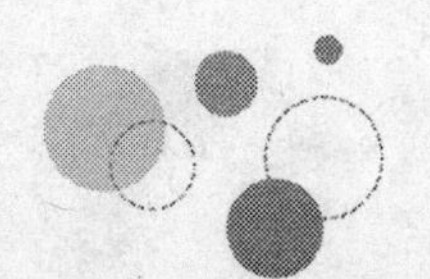



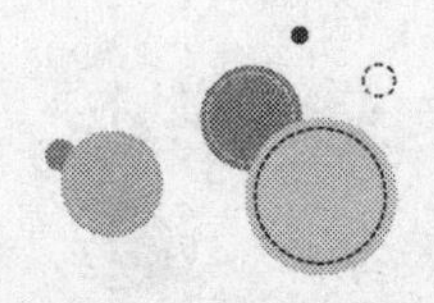

nodded to show that Tiffany would pay.

"*And* I've seen the rest of the contestants… not on my level," Miriam went on smugly. Of course she *hadn't* seen anyone else's costume, but Cleo didn't know that and Miriam loved to wind her up!

"What about Tiffany?" asked Cleo, nodding to Tiffany as she handed her her change.

Tiffany's eyebrows shot up and she looked curiously at Miriam to see what she'd say.

Miriam looked surprised, as if she hadn't even really considered Tiffany to be serious competition.

"Oh yeah, you'll get runner up," said Miriam matter-of-factly to Tiffany, waving her hand in the air like it didn't matter to her where Tiffany placed in the pageant. Deep down in her heart, Miriam truly believed that it *was* actually all about her!

Tiffany looked away hurt.

"But the rest," Miriam continued, "wallflowers… kind of like *you*," she finished unkindly.

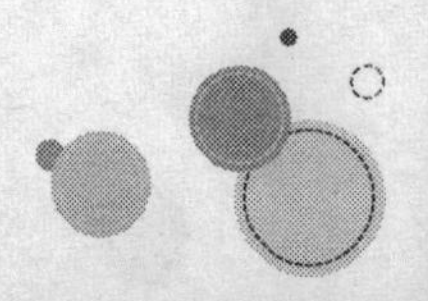

Cleo slammed the freezer lid shut and pasted on a fake smile; she didn't want Miriam to know how irritated she'd made her feel.

*I already feel like a bit of a frump in this stupid uniform, and she's not making my day any better!* Cleo thought grimly.

But her efforts to appear upbeat and unaffected were for nothing. Miriam and Tiffany had already gone and all that was left was an ice-cream wrapper that Miriam had carelessly dropped on the ground, and her last words, which still hung in the air.

Ten minutes later Cleo was back to her normal self. It was hard to stay angry when it was such a great day and she was surrounded by happy, smiley people.

Cleo often thought that it was one of the cool parts of her job, that she dealt with families out for a fun day, or couples on a date; people enjoying themselves!

*It's impossible to come to the marine park and have a bad time*, Cleo thought happily.

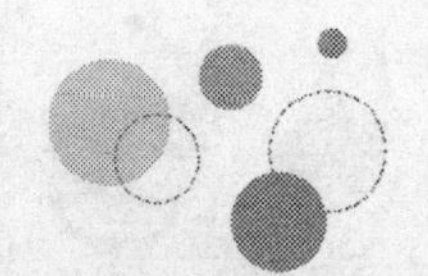

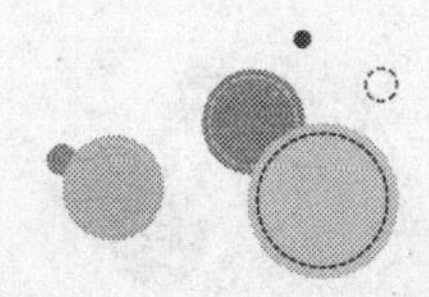

Just at that moment Mrs Geddes, Cleo's boss, came striding around the corner.

"Ahh, I've found you. Cleo darling, we're short staffed for the Miss Sea Queen Pageant, can you do nine to four?" she asked, all business-like.

Cleo thought for a minute – *Yes I could probably work that day, and I do need the money, but…*

"Actually, I *can't* work that day," she said apologetically. "I'd like to help but I've decided to enter the pageant."

Mrs Geddes looked at her in surprise. She'd been counting on Cleo, usually such a willing girl, to do the shift.

"Oh… *lovely*," Mrs Geddes smiled uncertainly. "Well don't you worry about it, I'll find someone else."

And with that she gave her a little wave and was gone.

Cleo looked at Mrs Geddes retreating back.

"What have I got myself into now?!" she said to herself.

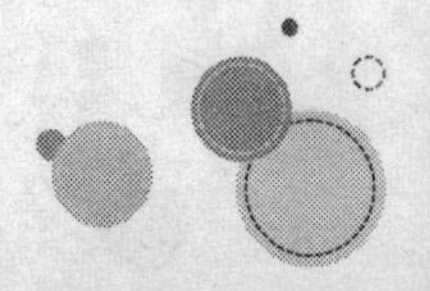

# Chapter 5

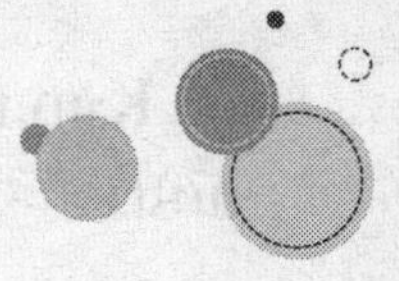

Kim walked home from the Juice-Net Café by herself, her head in the clouds the whole time as she ambled along the familiar streets thinking about Cleo's diary. Ever since she'd found the diary, Kim had wanted to talk to someone about it. She had a feeling her friends would have been horrified to find out she'd gone through Cleo's personal things, so they were out, but she couldn't think of anyone else to share her new-found knowledge with. Kim wasn't even sure what the diary meant!

The whole time she'd been at the Juice-Net Café with her friends that morning, she hadn't mentioned anything about it, although the diary was all she could think about. Even when some boys they knew from school came in, Kim's attention had been elsewhere. It was so obvious she had something on her mind that Danielle, Kim's best friend, had even asked her if she felt ill!

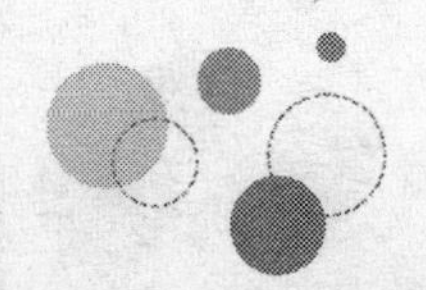



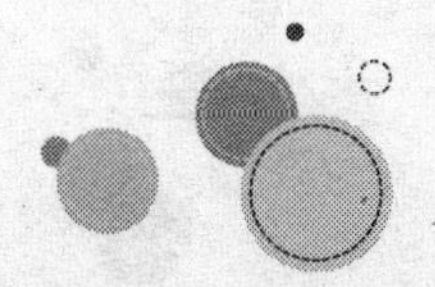

Kim used her key and let herself into the house.

She heard the radio on in the lounge room and went in to find her mum doing some ironing.

"Hi, love," said Mrs Sertori. "Did you have a nice time down at the café?"

"Yeah, it was fine," Kim answered distractedly.

"Are you alright, hon?" asked her mum, hearing something strange in Kim's voice.

*Should I say something?* Kim wondered. *But what exactly?*

"Mum," she began. "Do you think Cleo's being acting a bit… *different* lately?"

Mrs Sertori stopped what she was doing and thought for a minute.

"No, not particularly," she replied with a shrug. "What do you mean?"

"Like… like she might be in some kind of cult or something?" said Kim.

Mrs Sertori laughed and put the iron down. She had a feeling the conversation might be a

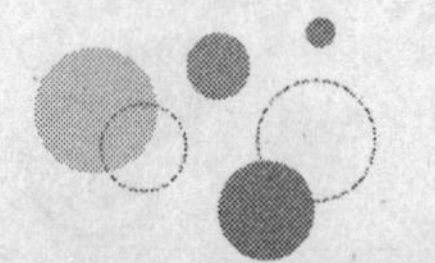



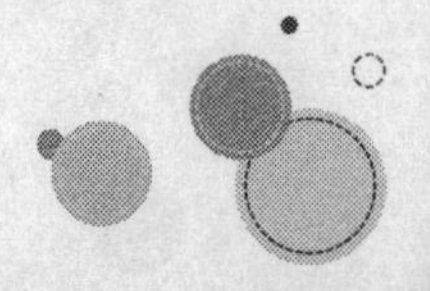

long and very odd one!

"Do you even know what a cult is, Kim?" she asked, wondering where her youngest daughter could have got such a strange idea.

"No. But I do know it makes people do weird things," said Kim, trying to sound knowledgeable.

But before her mum could say anything else, they heard the front door open and close as Cleo rushed into the room.

"Oh good, Mum, glad you're home," she said brightly, before adding. "This doesn't involve you Kim, so *scram*."

Kim stood her ground for a second. Cleo always bossed her around and she didn't like it! But if she left her mum and Cleo to talk... perhaps she might overhear something interesting.

Kim looked daggers at Cleo and stomped out of the room and up the hallway, but she only went as far as the bottom of the stairs before sneaking back to listen in.

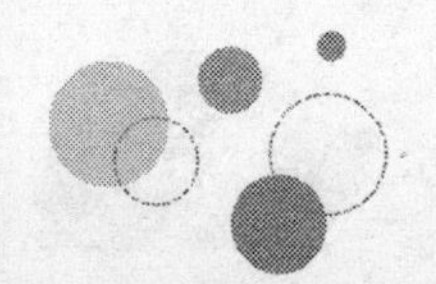



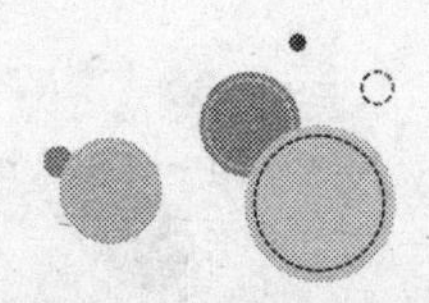

Cleo watched her go. *She is so painful!* she thought irritably, before she remembered what she'd rushed home for.

"Mum, you know how you've always wanted to teach me how to sew? Well, now would be a *really* good time. Like, not *right* now, I have fish that need me, but later on," said Cleo hurriedly.

Mrs Sertori looked confused. She was sure what Cleo was saying made sense in her own head, but it had come out of her mouth all in a muddle!

"Uh, *okay*," Mrs Sertori replied.

"That's great! I'll see you later then!" Cleo said delightedly and she ran out of the room.

Mrs Sertori sighed as she heard Cleo racing up the stairs to her room.

*What on earth has gotten into my girls?* she wondered. *First Kim and now Cleo?*

In the hallway, Kim looked equally confused. Cleo hadn't wanted to discuss secrets; she'd only wanted sewing lessons!

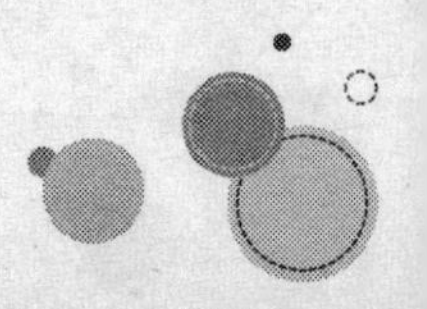

Kim checked that the coast was clear and tiptoed down the hall to Cleo's bedroom. She put the empty glass she was carrying against the door and listened carefully to the silence inside. Kim got lots of her ideas from the television and this glass-as-a-listening-device wasn't working out quite like she thought it would, because Cleo was *definitely* in her room and Kim couldn't hear a thing!

She rapped on the door and hurriedly walked in before Cleo could answer, hoping to catch her out doing something suspicious.

*How disappointing*, Kim thought, peering around the room, *there's Cleo and all she's doing is cleaning out her boring old tropical fish tank!* There had to be more going on than that! The creepy diary, Cleo's strange behaviour... why would *anyone* have their door shut if all they were doing was polishing the glass of their empty aquarium?

"Why are you always shutting your door?" Kim asked innocently, her eyes darting around the room looking for anything unusual.

"To keep you out," replied Cleo, all but

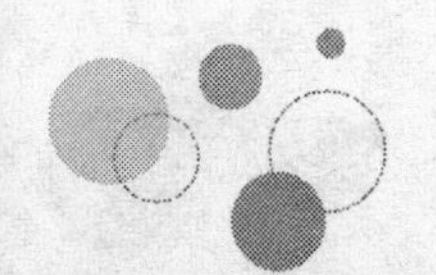



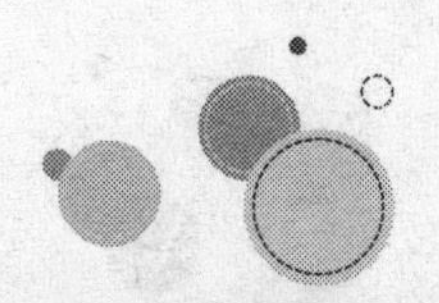

ignoring her. "Did I *say* come in?"

"Well… why do you *need* to keep me out?" Kim continued.

"Because you're annoying," Cleo replied, smiling sweetly. "Goodbye."

Kim was losing ground fast; this wasn't the way things worked out when Veronica Mars was investigating on the TV!

"What did you do with your fish?" Kim asked as Cleo continued polishing her empty tank.

"They're in the… bath," replied Cleo, gesturing with her head towards their shared bathroom.

That was all that Kim needed. Cleo's split-second hesitation before she replied told her that *something* fishy was going on and she hustled off importantly into the bathroom to find some clues.

Cleo breathed a sigh of relief and glanced up at the wobbly block of water, complete with tropical fish swimming gaily around inside, that she held hovering in mid-air with her powers. It

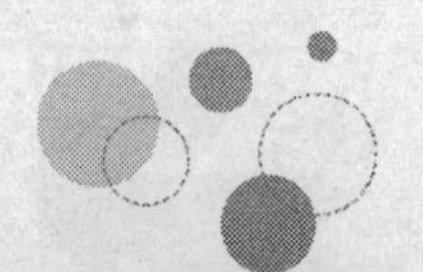



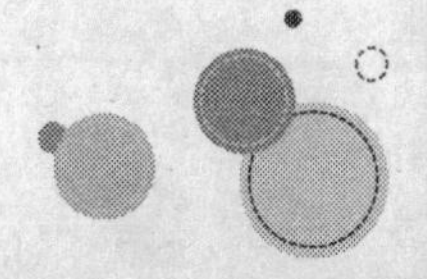

was much easier to scrub out the aquarium now that she had special powers over water!

*And with way less chance of getting splashed by water and turning into a giant fish myself*, thought Cleo grimly.

She had to be more careful though, particularly with Kim hanging around.

*Imagine if Kim had just looked up! How would I have explained* that*!* thought Cleo as she lowered the water safely back into the tank.

She could hear Kim in the bathroom; the squeak of the shower curtain being pulled back and the opening and shutting of doors and drawers. *She's really giving the room a good search!* Cleo thought.

Kim burst back into the room; she hadn't found any evidence in the bathroom to suggest anything unusual was going on, but then she hadn't found any *fish* either… Then Kim spotted the aquarium, complete with water and happy tropical fish!

"How did you *do* that?" asked Kim, wonderingly. "There was nothing in the bath!"

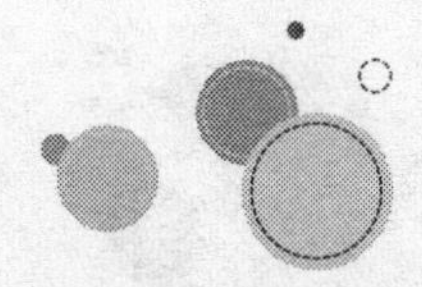

Cleo glanced over at her from the bookcase where she'd been tidying up.

"Did I say bath? I meant bucket," Cleo replied, catching sight of a bucket on the floor near the bathroom door.

Kim stared narrowly at Cleo; she knew something wasn't right. Cleo was such a terrible fibber and she was obviously lying now. If only Kim could find some proof.

With one last look around, Kim stalked out of the room, shutting the door behind her as Cleo watched her retreating back with a mixture of relief and suspicion. Kim was on to something, but Cleo couldn't quite figure out exactly what she knew, or *thought* she knew.

Kim sat on the couch with her knees up and the huge family atlas balanced on her lap.

She was supposed to be doing her homework, but when she thought no one was looking, she peered over the top of the massive book at Cleo's back as she sat working at the dining table.

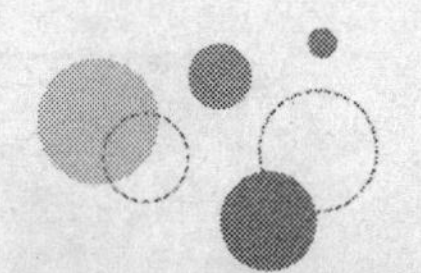

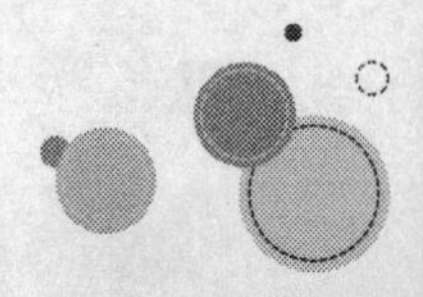

*What's she hiding?* Kim wondered as her eyes narrowed in thought.

Every now and again she turned a page, making it look like she really *was* studying, but all the while she had Cleo's diary hidden inside the pages of the atlas and was secretly trying to decipher the code that it was written in.

*I'm getting nowhere!* Kim thought, angry at herself. *I might have to get some help… I need someone who's good at maths or something…*

Unaware that she was the subject of Kim's detailed examination, Cleo sat innocently at the table and tried to think up ideas for her Miss Sea Queen costume.

*It can't be anything too complicated*, thought Cleo, *I don't have a lot of time; the contest is tomorrow!*

She looked around the kitchen for some inspiration.

*I could go as a pirate!* she thought, catching sight of the stripy t-shirt her mum was wearing as she prepared dinner. *No, it's a pageant, not a 'Pirates of the Caribbean' party!*

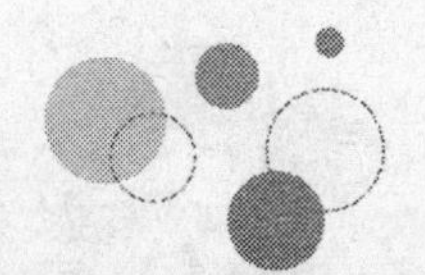



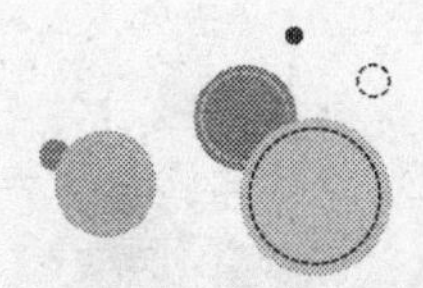

*Um, I could make a lobster outfit!? No, that's too hard. And I can't go as a mermaid! Emma and Rikki would go nuts!*

Cleo's mum watched her girls working on what *she* thought were their school assignments. *Such good girls*, she thought proudly, *always working hard.*

"What are you reading?" she asked Kim.

Kim almost jumped out of her skin! She'd been studying the drawings in the diary so intently she hadn't heard her mum come up beside her.

"Oh! Something for school," she replied, as she waved her hand around in a vague way. Kim had worked on her 'innocent look'; she knew if she slammed the book shut, she'd seem guilty and her mum would want her to explain exactly what she was doing and perhaps look over her work. But if she sat still and met her mother's eye, then her mum would probably leave her alone.

"It must be good," said mum happily.

Kim smiled up at her.

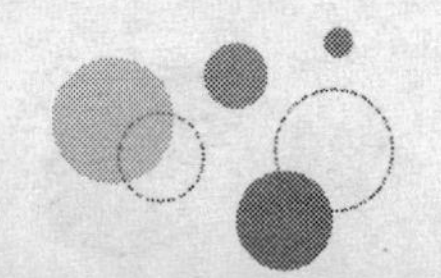



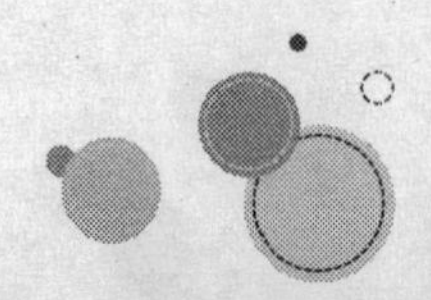

"It's *very* educational," she said, feeling much more sure of herself. *Yes, Mum, it's very educational, much, much more than* you *realize.*

Cleo's mum smiled back and patted Kim on the head. She had to admit she was a bit worried by Kim's behaviour. It was very unlike her to sit quietly on the couch and study.

Mum thought back to their earlier conversation, recalling how Kim had brought up Cleo's possible involvement in a cult. She glanced back at the cover of the atlas for a second. *Surely Kim isn't researching the best countries to go to if you want to* join *a cult?!* she thought suddenly.

She shook herself, realizing immediately what a stupid thought it was, and went back to the kitchen.

"Cleo, you'll have to pack up your things so Kim can set the table. It's almost tea-time," Mum said.

Kim groaned dramatically from the couch. Setting the table was one of her most hated jobs.

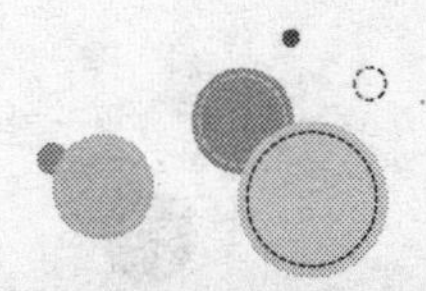

But Cleo wasn't listening. "Sure, Mum. In a minute," she said, as she continued staring dreamily into space.

*What about a… ship! I could put chopsticks in my hair and have a sail and a… oh, that's a moronic idea.*

Cleo's mum stood and looked over Cleo's sketches, which were spread out all over the table. She couldn't tell what any of them were meant to be!

*I hope Cleo's not going to embarrass herself in front of all those people tomorrow*, Cleo's mum thought nervously as she tidied up around Cleo; gathering her sketches up into a pile and scooping up her pencils and popping them back into her pencil case.

Suddenly Cleo sat bolt upright. *I've got it! I have the most perfect idea!* she thought excitedly.

Startled, Cleo's mother jumped in fright and knocked over Cleo's glass of water that was on the table.

"*Oooooooh*," moaned Cleo, as she sprung out of her chair. "What have you done?"

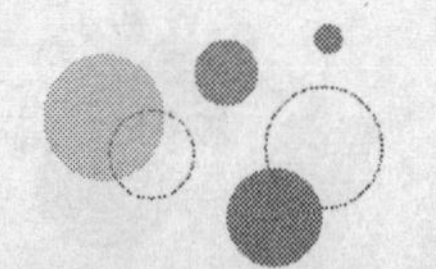



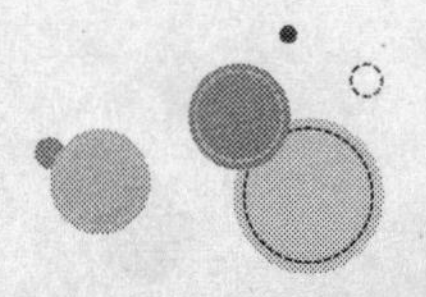

The water had splashed right across some of Cleo's sketches and a few stray drops had landed on her arm!

"It's only water, darling," her mother said, but Cleo was clearly upset as she ran out of the room.

This was exactly the kind of thing Kim had been waiting for; an opportunity too good to miss! Cleo had totally overreacted and Kim *had* to know why. She was on her feet in a second, and with Cleo only a few steps ahead of her, both girls raced down the hallway to the bathroom.

*I'm going to turn into a mermaid in front of my nosy sister!* thought the terrified Cleo as she flung open the bathroom door and skidded inside.

Three… two… one… she felt the familiar tingling as her feet disappeared from under her and she toppled over, her tail slapping loudly on the floor.

Kim reached the doorway half a second after Cleo but only had enough time to glimpse the coppery scales of Cleo's tail before the door

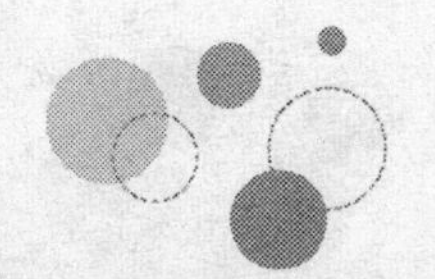



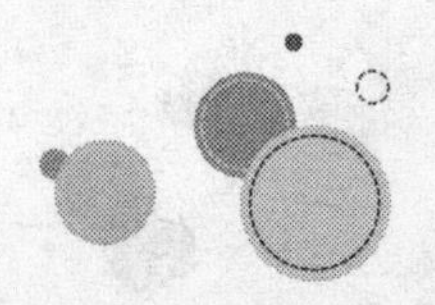

slammed shut with a bang.

Kim rubbed her eyes in disbelief. She couldn't believe what she'd just seen! Or more to the point, what *had* she just seen? She put her ear to the door, but inside everything was quiet.

"Kim!" her mother hissed angrily. "Get away from that door."

Reluctantly, Kim went back into the lounge room and picked up the atlas from where it had fallen on the floor. Luckily in her haste to rush after Cleo, she had slammed the atlas shut, so her mum wouldn't have had a chance to see the diary inside.

"I don't know what you think you're up to, but it's rude to listen at doors and your sister is obviously upset enough without you making things worse by poking your nose into her business," her mother said as she threw the ruined sketches into the sink and mopped up the spilt water.

But Kim was too busy studying one particular picture in the diary to listen; the one she thought was of Cleo and Emma swimming

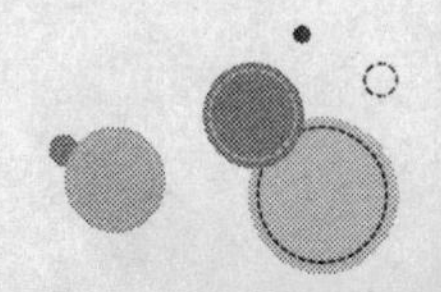

with dolphins. Kim nodded to herself; she needed help with this mystery and *now* she knew exactly whom she was going to ask for it…

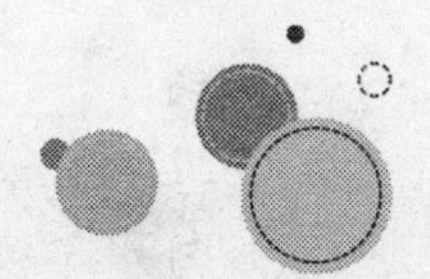

# Chapter 6

Later that afternoon, Emma's family were gathered at the dining room table playing cards. Every week they tried to do some kind of fun group activity, with everyone involved. When Emma had been busy with her swimming training, this had been one way to ensure that they all spent some quality time together as a family.

The doorbell chimed and Emma jumped up to answer it.

"Oh," said Emma with surprise. She hadn't been expecting any of her friends to call around and she certainly hadn't expected to see Kim, Cleo's little sister.

Her look of uncertainty must have been obvious.

"I came to see Elliot," said Kim quickly, ducking past Emma and walking into the house.

Elliot, on hearing his name, looked up from

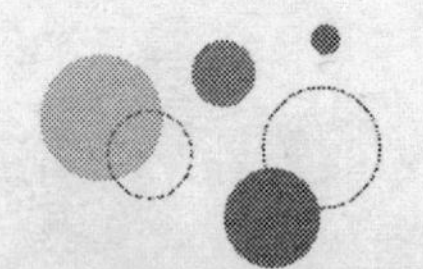



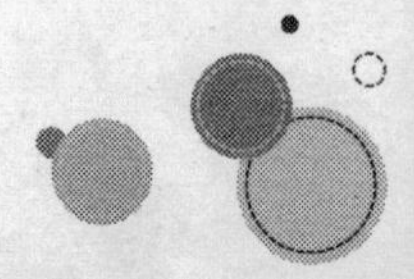

the hand of cards he was holding.

*Urgh, it's Kim from school,* he thought.

"What for?" Elliot asked irritably. It wasn't that he disliked Kim, but she could be a bossy know-all sometimes. Plus they weren't exactly friends either. Their sisters were friends of course and sometimes their parents would get together for a barbecue, but just because Kim and Elliot were the same age and had played together when they were little, people had just assumed they were good friends.

Emma smiled. *Elliot's all grown up and has got himself a little girlfriend*, she thought gleefully. Although if Elliot had had any idea what she was thinking he probably would have been horrified.

"I'm just going to go clean my room," said Emma innocently. *Leave these two young lovebirds to it,* she signalled to her parents with a toss of her head.

Emma's mum and dad jumped to their feet.

"We'll come and help," they said in unison, as they bustled out into the hallway.

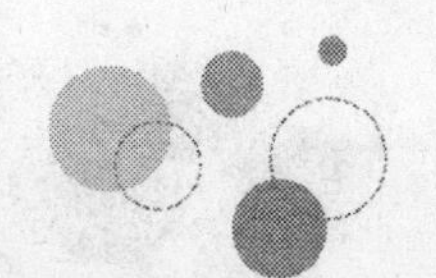



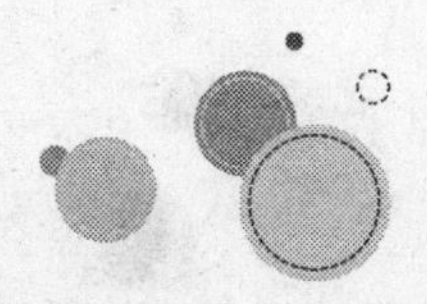

*This is just too adorable*, thought Emma's mum, squeezing her husband's hand. Emma's dad looked blankly at his wife. He had no idea what was going on, he just wanted to play cards!

Elliot eyed Kim suspiciously, waiting to see what she wanted. But Kim wasn't saying anything until Elliot's family were out of sight.

"*Yes?*" he asked expectantly, crossing his arms over his chest. He was just about to start tapping his foot impatiently, something he'd seen Emma do so successfully, when Kim peered over at the door to make sure the coast was clear before she sprung into action.

"Here," she said, as she pulled a book out from under her jersey and handed it to Elliot. "Read *this*, it's Cleo's diary."

Elliot recoiled in horror.

"I'm not reading someone else's diary," he said with disgust.

Kim merely rolled her eyes. She'd had a feeling that Elliot was going to take that tone.

*Just like his sister!* she thought, unkindly,

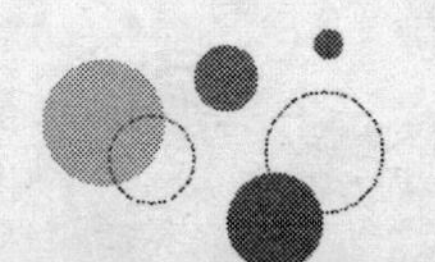

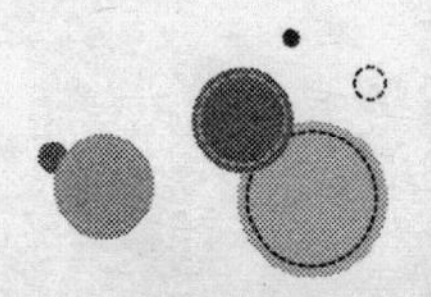

*They're all so Family Play Nice. I don't know how they can stand themselves!*

"It's for your own protection," said Kim, laying on the mystery as thick as she could as she shoved the diary at him again.

Elliot took another step back.

"It's *private*," he said, still refusing to take the diary.

Kim sighed. It was going to be harder than she'd thought! *Oh well, here goes nothing.*

"Listen, I have reason to believe that my sister, your sister and possibly Rikki are mermaids," said Kim bluntly. She shoved the book into his hands. "Read it."

Elliot reluctantly took the book and sat down. He'd play along with Kim if it meant he'd be able to get her out of the house quicker.

He opened Cleo's diary at a random page and flicked backwards through a few pages.

He saw some strange looking drawings of what appeared to be Emma, Rikki and Cleo and thought there was something wrong with

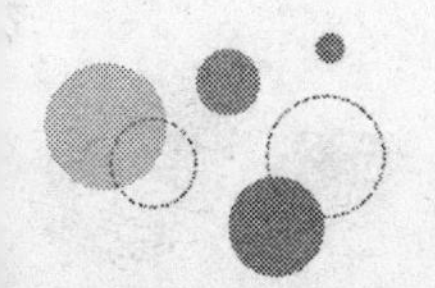



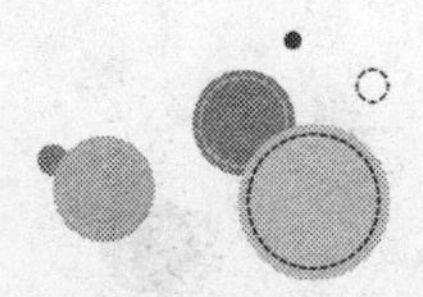

the way their legs were drawn, but he didn't know where Kim was getting the mermaids idea from.

Elliot studied the writing for a minute, but couldn't make any of the words out.

"It's in code," he said more to himself than to Kim.

Kim pulled a face.

"*So*? Its all there," she said with annoyance.

"It doesn't make any sense," said Elliot logically.

*He can be so thick! He should be grateful I'm willing to help him!*

Kim grabbed the diary back.

"But look at *this*… and *this*… and *this*…" said Kim, pointing to the drawings with her stubby fingers. "They're *mermaids.*"

But Elliot would need more evidence than a few drawings in a diary to convince him something was wrong with *his* sister.

"They could just be doodles," he said sensibly. "I like to doodle."

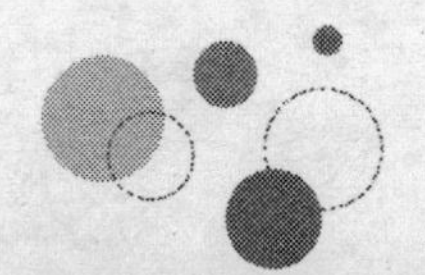



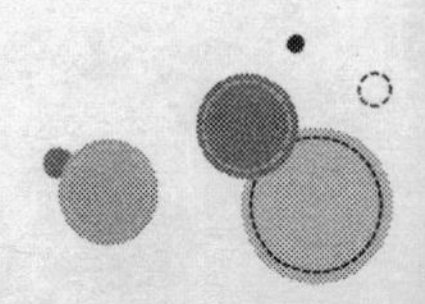

Kim tugged wildly at her hair with frustration.

"*Elliot!* I *saw* Cleo in our bathroom, *with a tail!* I know it might sound crazy, but if I'm right, they even have weird powers over water."

Suddenly Kim heard a door close and heard footsteps padding up the hallway.

As quickly as she could, she shoved the diary under one of the cushions on the couch and leaned on it innocently.

Emma appeared at the breakfast bar in the kitchen.

"Don't mind me, I'm just getting a drink," she said, smiling.

Elliot and Kim spun around to watch her, both of them grinning broadly as they tried to look guilt-free.

"She's a *freak*," Kim whispered coaxingly. "What's *she* gonna drink, huh? It can't be water, she can't touch the stuff."

Elliot turned and stared at Kim in shock. He was getting the feeling that she was beginning to enjoy herself. She could say what she liked

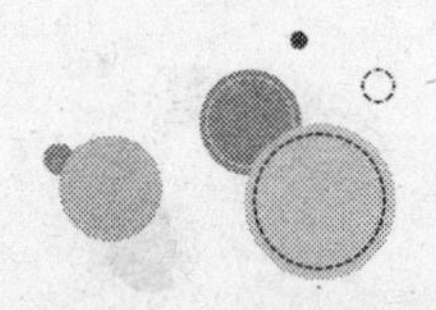

about her own sister, but no one was going to get away with being mean to *his* big sister.

Emma, meanwhile, unaware of what was going on, grabbed a bottle of water from the fridge, slipped a straw into it and left the kitchen.

When she was out of earshot, Elliot turned to meet Kim's level stare.

"You were saying?" he asked sarcastically.

But Kim had an answer for everything.

"She's smart." Kim said with begrudging admiration. "She drinks out of a bottle with a straw so she doesn't get water on her skin."

*Kim has an answer for everything*, thought Elliot, getting frustrated.

"I think you should leave now," he said, getting up off the couch.

"You've got to believe me," Kim pleaded.

Elliot snatched the diary out from under the cushion and thrust it into Kim's hand.

"See, that's the thing, I *don't*," said Elliot as he frog-marched Kim to the door.

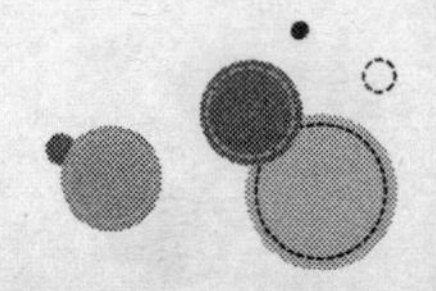

"Oh, listen, *please*," Kim pleaded. She needed Elliot on her side if she was going to try to get to the bottom of the mystery.

But Elliot wasn't persuaded.

"See you at school," he said mechanically, opening the door.

"Elliot, if you don't open your eyes and wake up to what's going on, you are going to be their first victim," said Kim desperately.

"See you at school," said Elliot as he pushed Kim out onto the step and shut the door.

Kim stood looking at the closed door. *If Elliot doesn't believe me when I've got such good proof*, she thought as her hand tightened around the diary, *what chance have I got of convincing anyone else?*

Inside, Elliot leaned against the door. *What's got into her?* he wondered. But then Elliot would have been the first person to admit to himself that he didn't know the first thing about girls!

Emma leaned against the bathroom door and

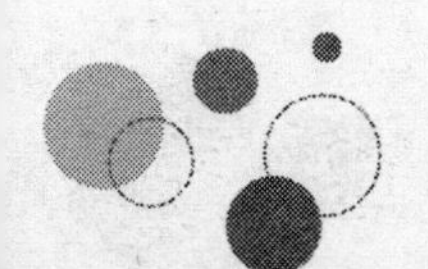



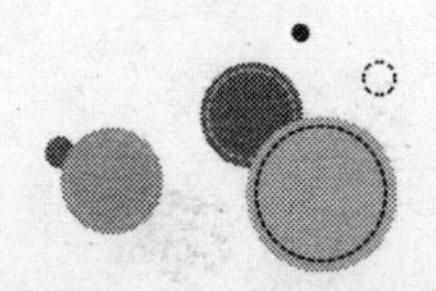

checked her watch for the third time.

"Elliot! *Hurry up*," she whined.

"I'll be out in a minute," Elliot called from behind the closed door.

Emma exhaled loudly. He'd said that five minutes ago, but Emma could hear the water still running. He was certainly taking his time in there.

"You've been in there for *twenty* minutes; there'll be no hot water left!" she snapped back crossly.

Elliot stuck his head right under the shower nozzle and felt the water wash over him. He could barely hear Emma's voice under the rush of the water, but he could sense that she was running out of patience.

Emma put her ear to the door, tapping her foot impatiently. *I can't* believe *he's still in there!* she thought with increasing frustration. *If there's no hot water left... I wonder how much* he'd *like it with no hot water!*

Elliot suddenly felt a sting on his neck. *What was that?* he asked himself. *And that? Hey!*

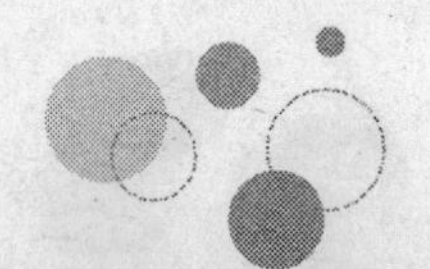



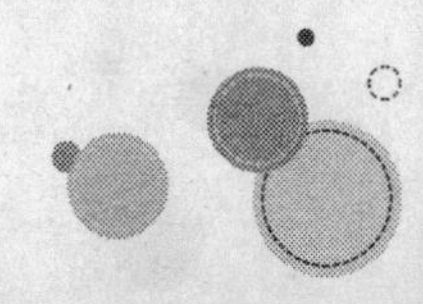

The water was more than cold; it was freezing.

*It's... ice!*

Elliot quickly jumped out, slammed the shower stall door and snatched his towel up.

*What's going on?!?*

He stood in the middle of the bathroom and shivered, more from shock than cold, before creeping back over to the shower and opening the door again. Inside it was hailing!

*There's a self-contained storm in my shower!*

Elliot quickly turned off the tap, making sure to keep his arm well away from the stinging hailstones, then carefully shut the door and looked around the bathroom to see if he could find any reason for the strange phenomenon.

"*Elliooooooot*!" Emma howled from the hallway, as she thumped on the door.

"Yeah, alright Em!" he yelled back grumpily.

*That's it! It's Emma!*

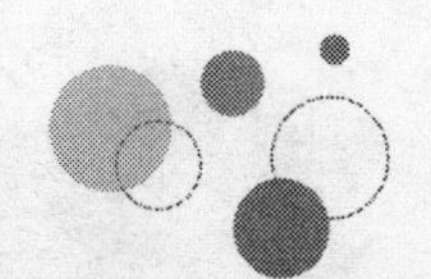



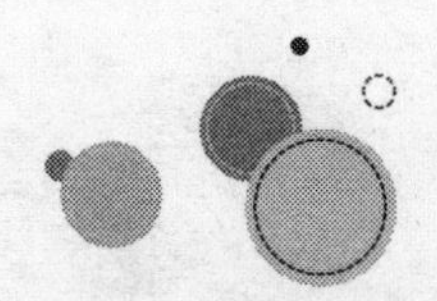

He stared at the closed door. He knew Emma was right on the other side of it and she was annoyed with him and she'd said that the shower would go cold and…

Suddenly Elliot felt *afraid*…

Later than night, once everyone was in bed, Elliot snuck downstairs and into the family room. Silently he lifted the telephone receiver and dialled a number.

"Kim, you were right about everything," he whispered quietly.

The next day Elliot raced through his chores. He'd already swept the driveway and tidied this room before the rest of the family were even up and it was still only 8.30 a.m.!

He was sitting at the breakfast bar eating cereal when his parents came down.

"Morning, champ," his dad said. "You were up early this morning."

"Yeah, I wanted to get an early start. I've got lots of things to do today," mumbled Elliot

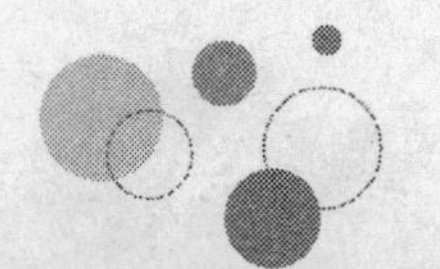

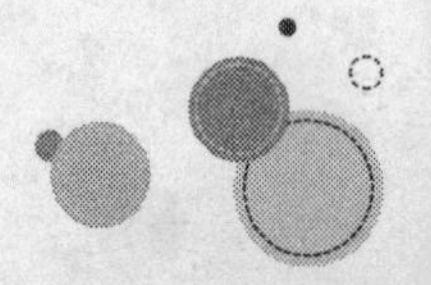

with his mouth full.

"Oh yes, like what?" asked his mother from the sink where she was filling the kettle.

"You know, *stuff*," Elliot replied awkwardly.

His parents rolled their eyes at each other – it's only going to get worse when he becomes a teenager, their look seemed to say.

Elliot fidgeted around in his chair. The last thing he wanted to do was keep secrets from his parents, but on the phone last night, Kim had been adamant. He was to tell no one about what had happened in the shower until he'd spoken to her first.

Elliot checked his watch. *If I'm going to meet Kim at 9.30 a.m. at the marine park, I better get going*, he thought as he jumped up from the table.

"Okay, I've gotta go and meet... some friends," he said. "I'll be home for lunch though, so I'll see you around one."

And with that Elliot scooped up his backpack from the back of the chair and left the house.

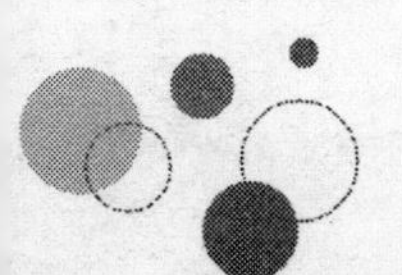



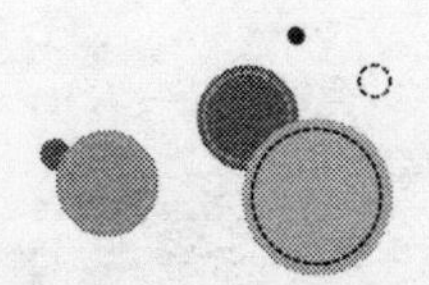

"One minute I was having a normal shower and the next thing I know it's hailing!" exclaimed Elliot, as he walked through the marine park with Kim.

They'd met up 15 minutes ago and he'd already told her the entire story twice.

"Ok, *calm down*," said Kim sensibly. She felt that perhaps Elliot was overreacting a bit. So he'd been hailed on in his shower; she'd actually seen her sister grow *a tail* and she wasn't freaking out like he was!

Kim pulled Elliot over to the side of the path to have a look in the polar bear enclosure.

"We have to figure out how to handle this properly," she said as she watched the polar bears eating their breakfast.

They stood silently, both deep in thought.

"Maybe we should talk to them," volunteered Elliot.

"*Talk*?? Are you insane?!" screeched Kim.

"Well, I was taught to resolve conflict with communication," replied Elliot, surprised by Kim's outburst.

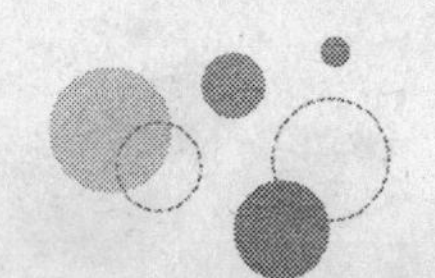



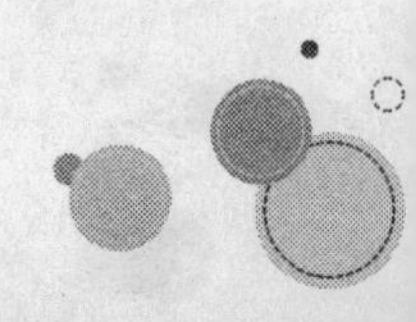

Kim let out a long-suffering sigh.

"Communication is for humans. They're *not* human. They're like..." she stopped and thought for a minute. "They're like... witches. *Vampires*. They can't be reasoned with... they *have* to be stopped."

"*How*?" asked Elliot, his eyes widening with fear.

Kim smiled. She had Elliot just where she wanted him.

"They take their true form when they're wet. I say, we *expose* them," she said delightedly. "We just have to pick our moment... and we'll be heroes."

Elliot had easily made it home in time for lunch and was just finishing the washing up when Emma came home and flopped down onto the sofa.

*It's a shame she didn't get home 10 minutes ago. I could've tricked her into helping me with the dishes. Then I'd have seen what happens when Emma gets her hands wet!* he thought.

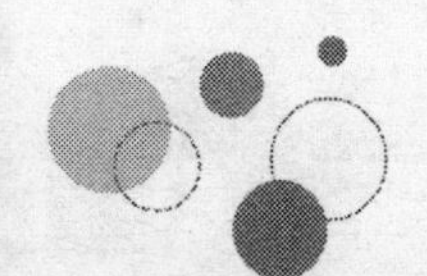



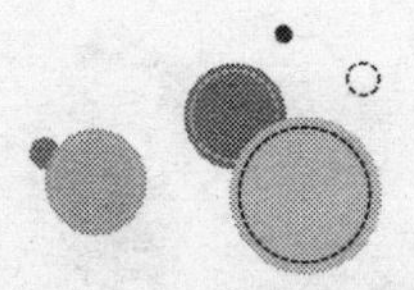

But Elliot felt guilty. It wasn't in his nature to sneak around spying on people and now here he was trying to prove his much-loved older sister was a mermaid!

But he had to know the truth!

Elliot filled a glass of water right to the brim and edged over to the sofa, holding the water out in front of him.

Emma looked up from the magazine she was reading and smiled.

"Hey, Elliot, what are you doing?" she asked.

"Nothing." Elliot's voice sounded strange to his ears. "What are you doing?"

"Just reading," Emma smiled again, not sensing anything odd.

The full glass felt heavy in Elliot's hand.

"Can I offer you some water?" he asked, shoving the glass in Emma's face.

Emma recoiled back as the water slopped up the side of the glass and almost spilt.

"No thanks," she replied, trying to keep her voice calm.

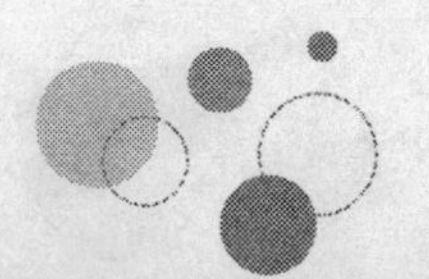



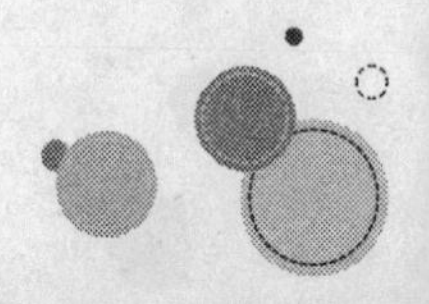

"I'm happy to share," Elliot persisted as he took a large gulp of water.

Emma looked at Elliot suspiciously – *something is definitely wrong here*, she thought with growing alarm.

"I'm not thirsty," replied Emma, although her mouth did suddenly feel dry with fear.

Elliot swallowed. He knew that Emma knew he was up to something and ordinarily she would have asked him straight out why he was acting so weird.

Instead, just as Elliot had feared, Emma was keeping something from him and it was something massive.

"In fact, I share *everything* with you, because you're my sister and all I get in return is secrets and lies," he blurted out, feeling suddenly very near to tears.

Emma stared up at Elliot in confusion. "What lies?" she asked in a shaky voice.

But inside Emma felt sick with the knowledge that Elliot had found out their secret.

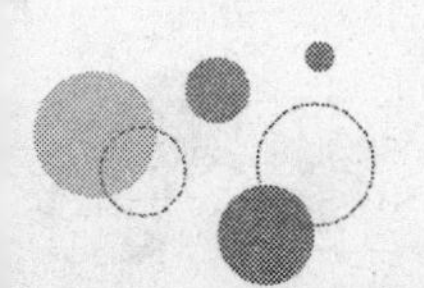



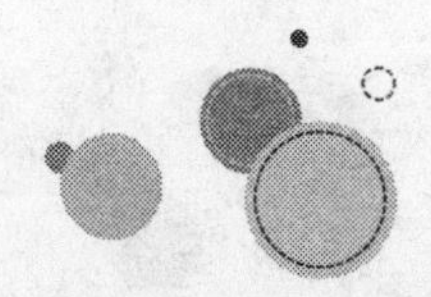

"Why didn't you *tell* me you were a mermaid?!" he howled, shoving the water even closer to Emma's face.

"Why would you think I was a *mermaid*?" asked Emma, faking a half-laugh to try and show Elliot that he was being silly.

"*Why*?!" Elliot banged the glass of the water on the coffee table and collapsed in a heap on the sofa. "Because when Kim came over yesterday she brought her sister's diary with her! There's pictures of you and Rikki and… and… and *you've got tails*!"

Elliot buried his face in his hands and sobbed.

Emma hated to see him so upset. They were a close-knit family and it had been so stressful on her keeping such a life-changing secret from them all that she felt like crying as well!

*But what good would that do?* Emma thought, pulling herself together a little. *Elliot's a kid and if I told him the truth, well it wouldn't be a secret for very long!*

She put her arm around Elliot's shoulders

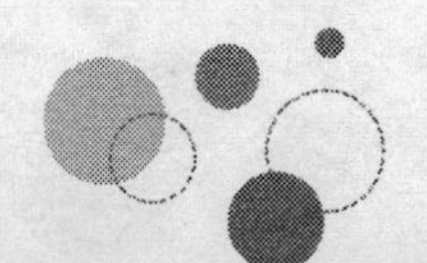



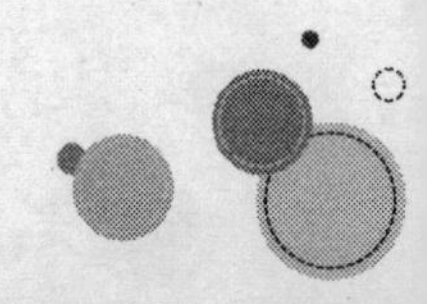

but he violently shrugged it off and jumped to his feet.

"So you're not denying it?" Elliot spat out, his face red and angry looking.

"I... I..." began Emma, but Elliot ran from the room before she could say anything more.

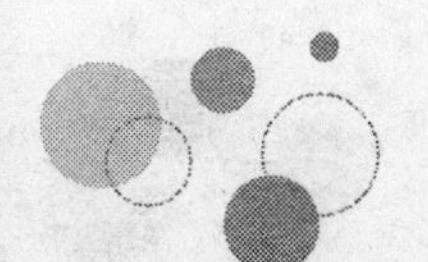



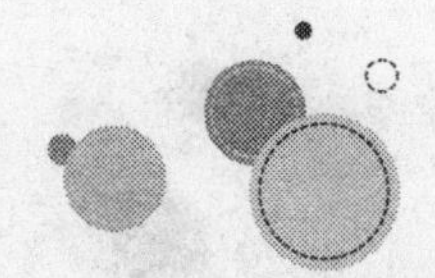

# Chapter 7

Emma was glad she'd walked over to Cleo's place and not taken her bike, because by the time she was at Cleo's door, she felt *a lot* calmer. She didn't want to have a massive screaming row with Cleo about writing a diary – Emma felt her blood pressure rise at the thought of it – but Cleo needed to be told how careless she'd been!

Emma took a deep breath and knocked on the door.

She only hoped that Kim didn't answer it, because Emma couldn't be held responsible for her actions if she saw that little… *deep breath, Emma*, she thought again and exhaled loudly.

Mrs Sertori opened the door with a smile.

"Hello, Emma," she said. "How are you? How's your mother?"

"She's fine, thank you, Mrs Sertori," said Emma pleasantly.

"I suppose you're looking for Cleo? She's in her room; go right up," said Mrs Sertori as she opened the door wider to let her in. "*Cleoooooo*, Emma's here," she yelled up the stairs as Emma ducked past her.

Emma mounted the stairs and wondered how she was going to bring up the subject of the diary with Cleo. All the way over she'd been too busy fuming to think rationally and now that she was here...

She knocked on Cleo's closed bedroom door and opened it.

Cleo was lying on her bed sketching.

"Hey," she smiled lazily in greeting. "How are you?"

"Are you crazy? You wrote a *diary*?" Emma blurted without warning as she slammed the door shut.

Cleo sat up in surprise; her mind whirred.

The two girls had been best friends for so long, there was no need for Emma to say anything more, Cleo knew *exactly* what she was talking about.

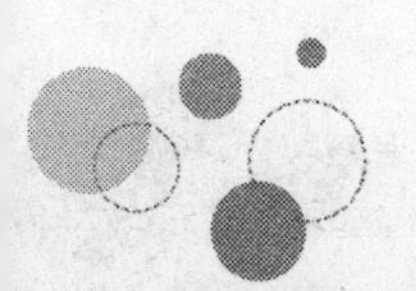



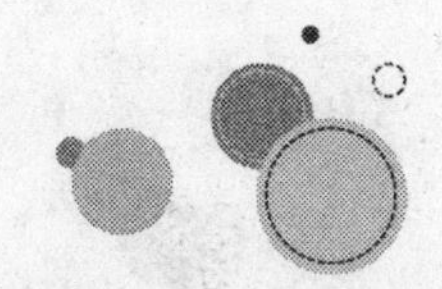

*Oh oh...*"Just a little one," she replied sheepishly.

*Just a little one...*Emma's head swam with rage as she recalled Elliot's tear-stained face.

"With *every* little detail of our mermaidness," she replied coldly.

The only outer sign of Emma's absolute fury was a tightening of her jaw, but that was enough for Cleo.

"I'd never let anyone *see* it," said Cleo, feeling a little annoyed herself. *As if I would!*

She got up off her bed, yanked open a dressing table drawer and began to search through her things.

She'd show Emma that she was more careful than she was given credit for.

*I'm being totally underestimated!* thought Cleo angrily. *It was here yesterday because I drew that really cool picture of me swimming with dolphins. Or was that the day before?*

Of course the diary wasn't where Cleo had hidden it at all. With her back to Emma, Cleo hastily pulled open another drawer. It wasn't in

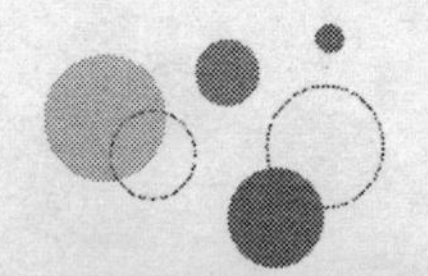



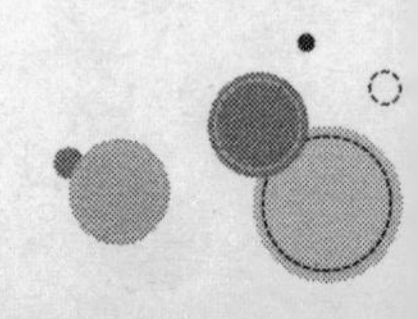

there either!

It was time to face facts.

"It's *gone*," said Cleo, ashamed.

"Yes I *know* it's gone! How do you think I found out about it? Your sister came around to my place yesterday and showed it to my brother!" Emma threw up her hands in frustration.

"Oh, I'm so sorry, Emma," replied Cleo apologetically, before quickly adding. "What are we going to do?"

"I don't know," said Emma quietly.

Now Cleo *was* worried; Emma always knew what to do.

"What if I try and find the diary?" Cleo suggested, trying to make amends. "I know most of Kim's hiding places so it shouldn't be too difficult."

Emma looked at her with surprise. She couldn't remember Cleo ever suggesting a solution to a problem. She usually waited for Emma to tell her what to do.

*She must feel really terrible about this*,

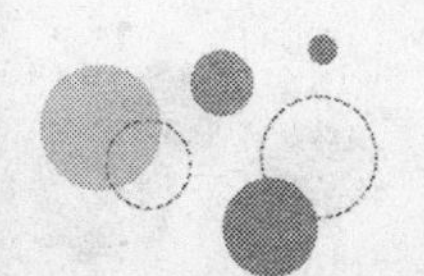



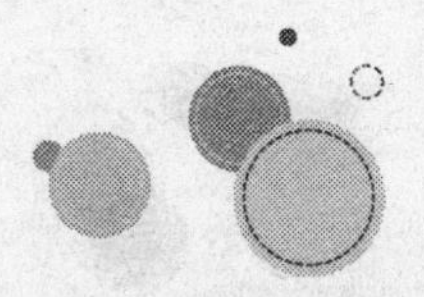

thought Emma, her anger decreasing.

"Okay, you find the diary and I'll call Rikki, because this affects all of us," said Emma. "We'll meet you at the Juice-Net Café later this afternoon?"

Cleo smiled with relief; Emma had forgiven her.

"Yeah, that's a good idea. I'll text you when I've found the diary."

"Okay, good. And Cleo? I'm sorry that I was so angry with you before, but if you'd seen Elliot's face, well you'd know why I…"

"Hey look, it's okay Emma," Cleo interrupted. "I know you're upset about keeping secrets from your family. I'd be angry at me too!"

The girls smiled at each other, all the tension between them gone.

"I'd better get going," said Emma in her normal voice. "I'll see you later."

After Emma had closed the door behind her on her way out, Cleo sat down on the edge of her bed and with her head in her hands, and

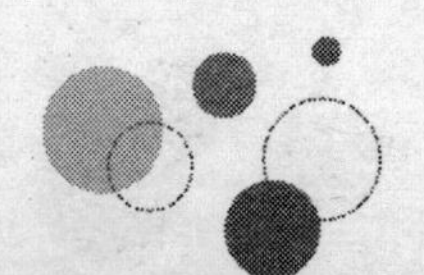



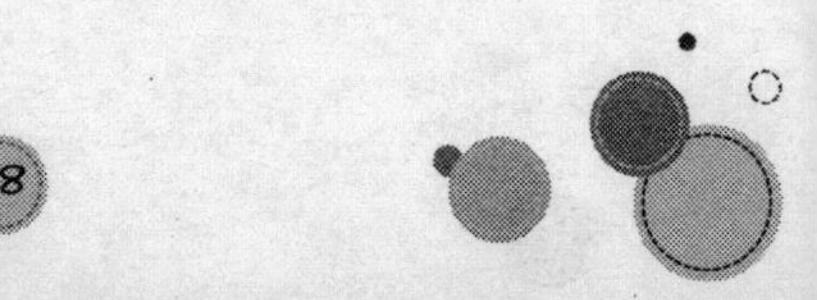

thought about where to start looking for the missing diary.

*I can't believe that Kim would come snooping around in my room!* she thought with disgust. *What am I saying? Of course I can believe it! It's exactly the kind of dirty trick she would pull!*

Cleo heaved herself angrily to her feet, marched to her bedroom door and flung it open. *"Kiiiiiiiiiiiiiim!"* she yelled, checking to see if her sister was at home.

Not hearing any reply, Cleo stomped heavily down the hallway to Kim's room and wrenched open her door. "Kim!" she repeated.

*Either Kim's ignoring me or she isn't home*, thought Cleo as she scoped out her sister's room. *And right now I don't care which it is, because I'm going through her things and I don't care if I do get caught!*

Downstairs Mrs Sertori heard Cleo yelling for Kim. *Oh dear*, she thought, *what's Kim done now?*

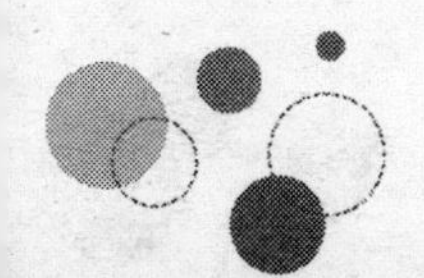

Two hours later Cleo walked through the door of the Juice-Net Café and saw Rikki and Emma sitting in a booth talking quietly together. Both girls looked up and gave her a little wave as she came in.

Cleo felt sick with guilt. *If only I hadn't written that stupid diary. Now everyone knows what an idiot I've been! I feel like a complete fool!*

But Cleo knew she couldn't put off facing up to her friends any longer. She knew they'd forgive her eventually – that's what friends do.

As she weaved her way through the tables she passed Miriam and Tiffany, with their heads together, deep in conversation, before noticing Lewis sitting at one of the internet terminals where he was deeply engrossed in whatever it was that Lewis did.

Cleo flopped down in the booth next to Emma and came straight to the point.

"I found the diary. It was under Kim's pillow," said Cleo matter-of-factly, her head bowed.

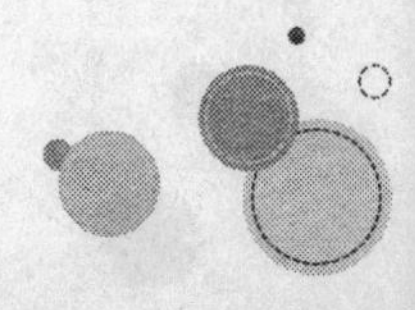

Emma had already filled Rikki in on what had happened and as Cleo spoke, both girls could see the mixture of anger and guilt on Cleo's face.

"Well at least you have it back," said Rikki reassuringly.

Cleo looked up to see Emma and Rikki nodding at her encouragingly and she immediately felt a bit better.

The beaded curtain of the Juice-Net café rattled noisily as Kim and Elliot, who had a black backpack slung over his shoulder, wandered in and looked around.

With one eye always on the door, Rikki was the first to spot them.

"Check out who's here," she said with a toss of her head.

Cleo exhaled noisily. "I'm going to *maim* her," she said, trying to push past Rikki and get to her feet.

"Just ignore them," said Emma sensibly as she gestured for Cleo to sit down again.

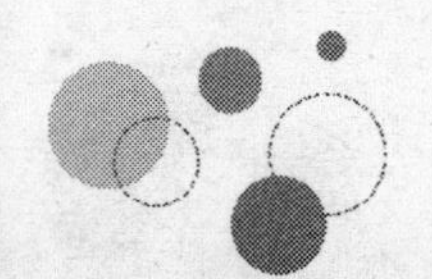



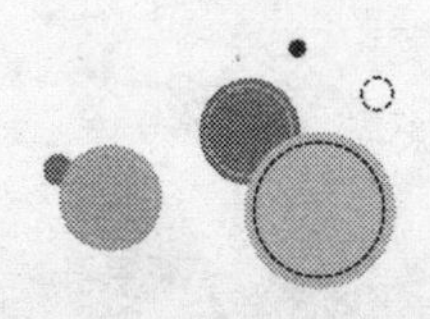

*The last thing we need is a public fight between two sisters!* she thought gloomily. *It'll only take Kim a second to accuse Cleo of being a mermaid and with Miriam and Tiffany sitting right there… oh that's* exactly *what we don't want to happen!*

She glanced over at them furtively, but neither Tiffany nor Miriam seemed to notice the tension in the air.

Over on the other side of the café, Elliot and Kim sat down at a vacant table and Elliot shoved his backpack onto the spare chair beside him.

"They're all here," said Kim gleefully as she surveyed the scene. "Did you bring the gear?"

Elliot grinned at her and reached over, pulling his backpack half open to show her what was inside.

In his bag was the largest super-soaker water pistol that Kim had ever seen. *This is going to be good!* she snickered to herself.

Emma glanced over at Elliot. She could tell

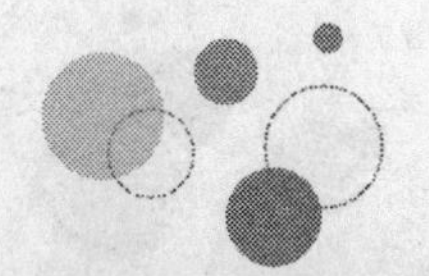



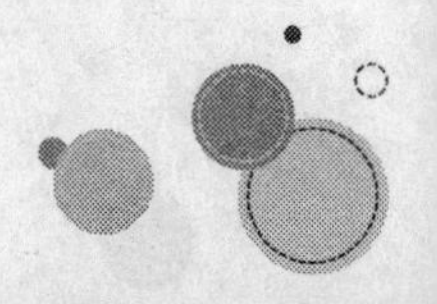

by the look on his face that he and Kim had something planned.

"They're not going to let this go," she said in a defeated tone, letting her head drop wearily into her hands.

Rikki looked at Emma with surprise. She'd never heard Emma sound so beaten.

"We've got to do something about it," she said, thumping the table determinedly, trying to rally her friends.

But the girls simply looked at each other, stumped for ideas. After a few moments of gloomy silence, Emma looked up with a hopeful expression as if something had just occurred to her. "Ahhhhh, *Lewis*?" she called out sweetly.

Lewis looked up from the computer screen and frowned.

"Hmmm?" he replied sceptically. He was all too familiar with Emma's *can-you-do-us-a-favour?* tone by now.

Emma wiggled her eyebrows and indicated with a nod of her head that she needed to talk

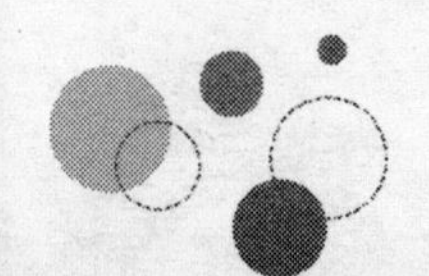



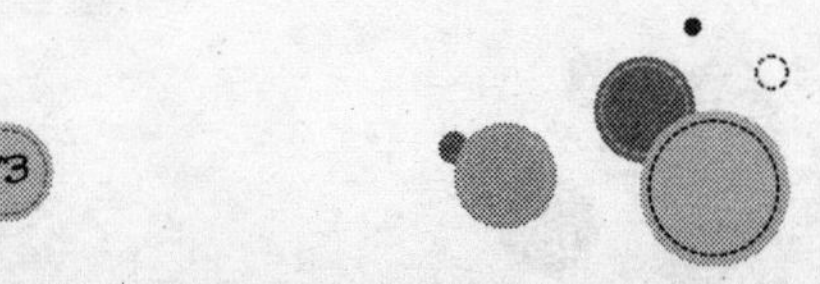

to him at the table.

Lewis sighed loudly. *Lewis to the rescue… again*, he thought as he pushed back the computer chair.

Meanwhile, Elliot was struggling to get the super-soaker out of his backpack. The long barrel had snagged on an inside pocket.

*This never happens in the movies,* he said to himself in frustration as he heard the lining tear inside the pack.

Suddenly Kim caught sight of Emma's signal to Lewis. "Wait," she barked at Elliot. "Lewis is one of them too."

Elliot stopped what he was doing and looked at Kim like she was crazy.

"I can't see *Lewis* as a mermaid," said Elliot earnestly.

"No, you *dork*, he'd be a merman. Like a boy-mermaid," she answered distractedly, her gaze still fixed on Lewis as he reluctantly got up from the computer and joined the girls in their booth.

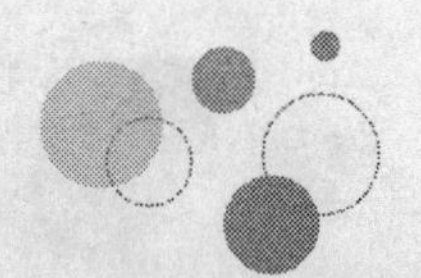

"Just sit tight," Kim ordered Elliot as he dropped the bag back under the table.

Lewis screwed up his face in pain as Emma gave him a brief run-down of the entire story up to that point. "How *much* do they know exactly?" he asked, looking at each girl in turn.

All three of them looked ashamed.

"Pretty much everything," mumbled Rikki, making sure not to look directly at Cleo. She knew how bad she already felt about all of this and didn't want to make things any worse.

"Oh that's great, that's perfect, well done!" said Lewis as he gave them a teasing round of applause.

"There's no need to be mean about it. It's done, okay? They know, so let's stop beating ourselves up over it and *do* something," said Rikki sensibly. "What's the plan, Brains?"

Tiffany looked up from her magazine and nudged Miriam, rolling her eyes towards the

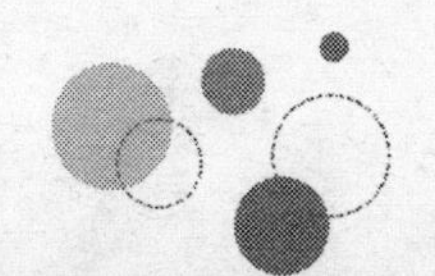



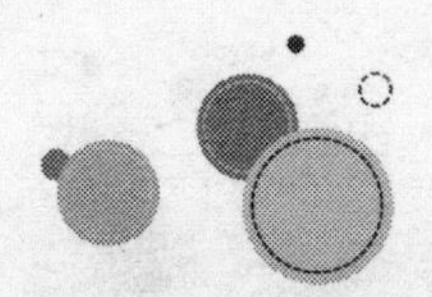

booth where Rikki, Emma and Cleo sat arguing with Lewis.

Miriam's eyebrows shot up as she took in the scene. "Trouble in paradise?" she asked with a giggle.

"Wanna hear something *hilarious*?" said Tiffany, leaning in towards Miriam to avoid being heard.

Miriam nodded her head excitedly.

"*Cleo* entered Miss Sea Queen," said Tiffany, thrilled to be the first person with the news.

Miriam's jaw dropped.

"*Noooo*! Imagine trying to pull a costume together overnight!" she said, her voice full of horror at the idea. If anyone knew how hard it was to successfully plan and execute a pageant outfit, it was Miriam. It made her sweat just *thinking* about the work involved!

Tiffany nodded her head in understanding.

"So *that's* what they're stressing about," she said with a smile.

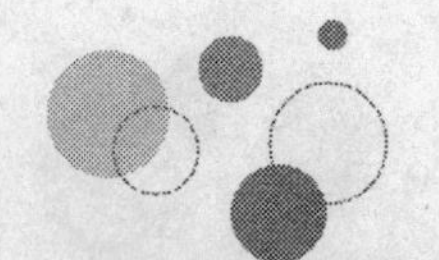



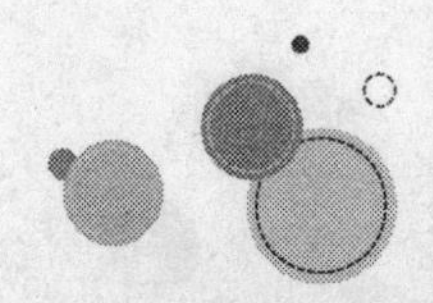

Lewis looked at Rikki; for once he had to agree with her, what's done was done. From here on in they had to think up solutions, not waste time laying blame.

"I think the best idea is to try and put them off the scent. Get them to think the diary is about someone else," said Lewis.

"Like who?" asked Cleo excitedly, pleased with the plan.

But Lewis hadn't thought quite that far ahead yet. He looked around the café for inspiration. It didn't take long before his eyes eventually set upon Miriam.

"Hey Miriam," he called out cheerily, giving her a wave at the same time.

Miriam looked up, confused, but Lewis wasted no time sliding out of the booth and strolling casually across to her table. She gave Tiffany a doubtful glance as he approached.

From their position on the other side of the café, Kim and Elliot watched as Lewis sat himself down at Miriam's table.

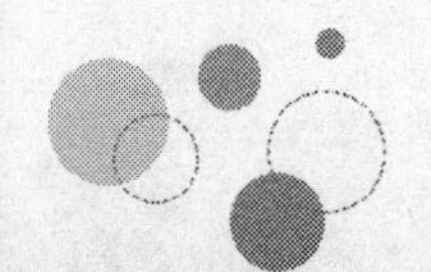



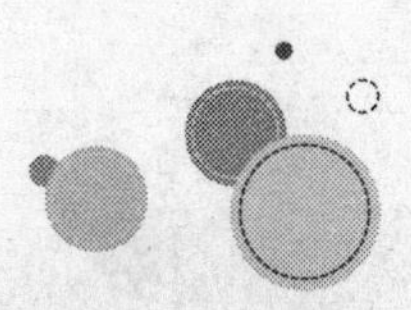

Kim inhaled sharply and her eyes grew wide with disbelief.

"*More* of them!" she whispered to Elliot, implying that Miram and Tiffany were mermaids too. "This is bigger than I thought!"

Lewis pulled up a chair and made himself comfortable.

"Why are you talking to me? You *never* talk to me," said Miriam, looking down her nose at him.

Following Lewis's lead, Cleo had tailed him closely and arrived at Miriam's table just in time to hear her question. "That's *silly*," she scoffed in reply. "We *like* you…"

Miriam peered suspiciously from Cleo to Lewis and back again. *There's definitely some funny business going on here*, she thought warily, *and I'm pretty sure I know what's causing it.*

"Don't think I don't know you've entered the contest, Cleo," Miriam sneered. "I know everything."

"You *do*?" Cleo asked, batting her eyelashes.

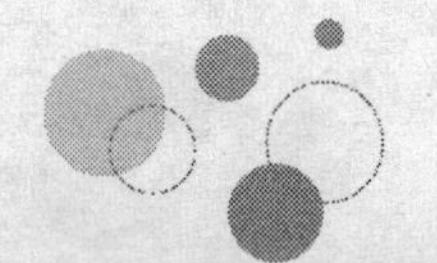



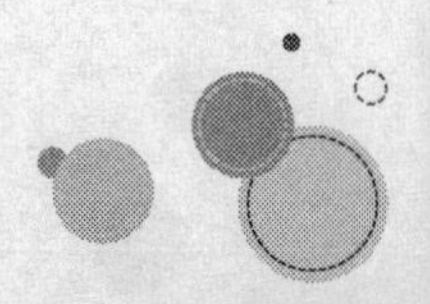

Emma and Rikki heard the challenge in Cleo's voice and quickly rushed over to join them all at Miriam's table, as if they intended to stop Cleo saying something she might regret later.

"Oh, *okay*," said Emma as she put her hands on Cleo's shoulders and directed her towards the door. "Let's go."

"What do you think *that* was about?" Elliot asked Kim as he watched his sister shove Cleo and Rikki out the door and onto the footpath.

"I don't know," said Kim thoughtfully. "But I do know there's a whole *coven* of mermaid creatures and we can't fight them in here."

Elliot nodded his head silently in agreement.

Lewis watched Kim and Elliot eagerly to see if they'd fallen for the trap he'd laid for them. Did they think that Miriam was a mermaid too? He needed another tactic, just to be sure – something that would convince them once and for all that the diary they'd found wasn't about Rikki or Emma or Cleo.

Lewis got up from the table, overbalancing

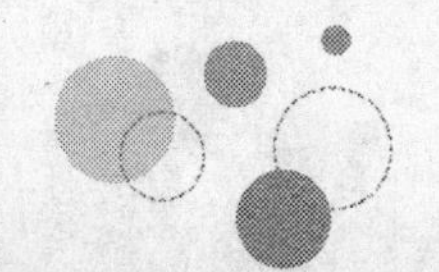



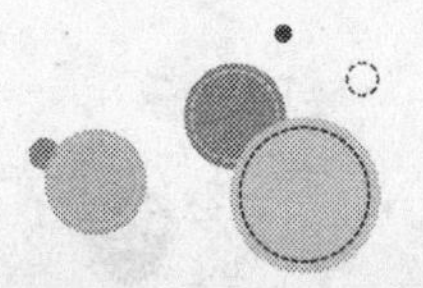

his chair and sending it crashing loudly to the floor.

"What a dork," said Miriam, causing a few people who sat near them to laugh.

But Lewis had knocked over the chair on purpose and he'd achieved his goal; everyone looked over and that *included* Kim and Elliot.

When he was sure all eyes were on him, Lewis went over to the computer that he'd been using before he'd joined the girls in the booth.

He felt four sets of eyes bore into the back of his head as he sat down and opened up the mermaid myths homepage he'd been reading earlier, scrolled down the page and then shut it down again. He then strolled casually over to the counter to pay for his time.

*And the trap is set*, he thought, feeling exactly like a criminal mastermind!

Tiffany and Miriam watched as Lewis swished the beaded curtain aside on his way out and looked at each other questioningly.

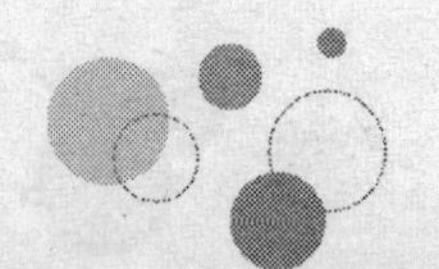



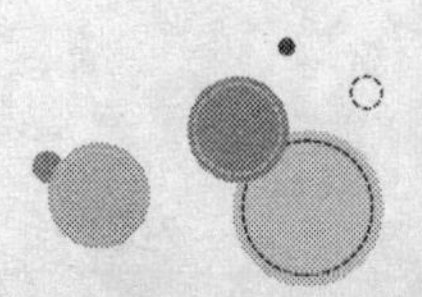

"Something's going on here," said Tiffany.

"Yeah, that Cleo has got something up her sleeve," said Miriam as she stared at the computer Lewis had just vacated. "I'm just not sure what..."

Miriam jumped to her feet and went over to the computer, which now displayed the Juice-Net Café homepage.

She clicked the 'history' tab onscreen and the mermaid myths homepage opened immediately.

"*Mermaids?* Cleo's entering Miss Sea Queen dressed as a mermaid? Ha!" Tiffany snorted dismissively. "Your idea is *way* better!"

But Miriam didn't see it that way. Her idea was a good one, but this... this was better!

"Shut up, Tiffany," she snapped. "Come on."

Miriam turned and marched back to their table, grabbed her bag and stormed out of the café. She didn't have much time if she was going to completely revamp her costume in time for the pageant.

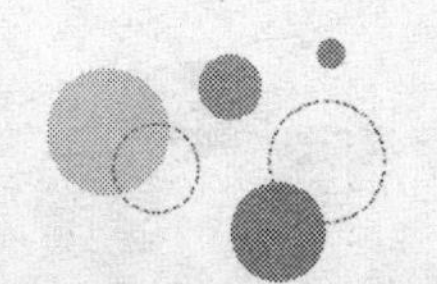



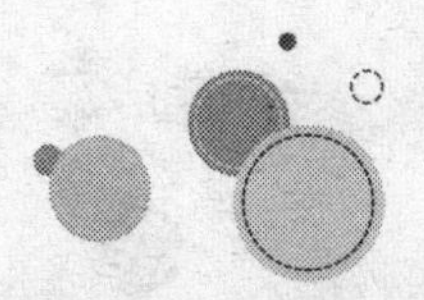

Even before the curtain on the door had finished swinging behind Miriam and Tiffany as they rushed out of the café, Elliot and Kim had raced over to the computer.

They stared in disbelief at the mermaid myths homepage.

"*Of course*!" Kim exclaimed. "It all makes sense now! Miriam is the *leader*."

Elliot looked at her doubtfully.

"You think so?" he asked.

Kim looked at him with pity.

"Duh! Miriam's *always* the leader," she replied.

*They're not trying very hard to keep it a secret!* she thought, *But I suppose they know that we know, so what's the point?*

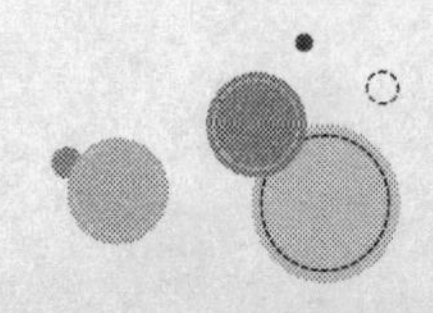

# Chapter 8

Miriam and Tiffany walked down to the marina. It was a short cut to Miriam's house from the Juice-Net Café and they were in a hurry.

"I need to pull another costume together overnight. It's big, but I can do it," said Miriam, full of confidence.

"Of *course* you can," agreed Tiffany enthusiastically.

"I need to stand out from the crowd. I need a hook… oh *hang on*! That's it! I've just had the most amazing idea!" said Miriam as she caught sight of a lone fisherman.

From an empty office overlooking the marina, the three girls watched as Miriam and Tiffany struck up a conversation with a man fishing off the jetty. They couldn't hear what was being said, but it looked like Miriam was asking the

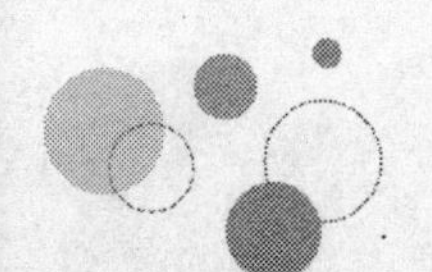



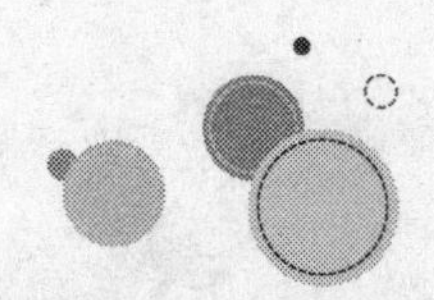

guy for something…

Kim and Elliot squatted down behind one of the many 44-gallon drums that littered the marina and kept a close eye on Miriam and Tiffany.

"What is she doing now?" whispered Elliot.

Miriam had rushed out of the Juice-Net Café with such a determined look on her face that they'd decided it would be sensible to follow her.

"She's putting a fisherman under her spell," answered Kim in a low voice, dreading the worst.

"Thanks *so* much," Miriam smiled charmingly at the fisherman as he handed over two of his fishing lures.

"No problem," he said, looking slightly confused as the two girls walked on.

"Cool," squealed Miriam, pleased with herself. "These will go great with my new outfit."

"What are they?" asked Tiffany curiously.

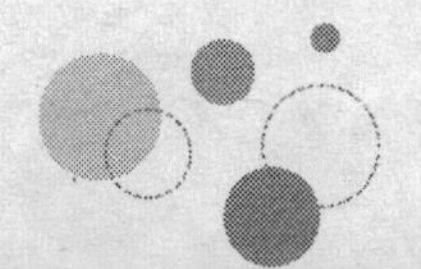

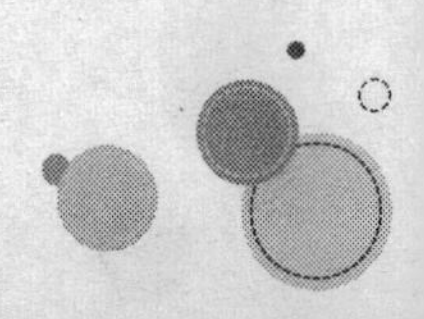

"Duh! *Accessories*," Miriam replied, holding the two flashing silver lures up to her ear lobes.

Tiffany blushed with embarrassment.

*I wish Miriam wouldn't try and make me feel like an idiot all the time!* she thought sadly.

But Miriam hadn't even noticed she'd hurt Tiffany's feelings; she'd suddenly spotted Kim and was already striding over to where she saw the kids hiding, her hair streaming behind her.

Kim and Elliot hunkered down a little lower behind the drum in the hope they hadn't been seen.

"You're Cleo's little sister aren't you?" Miriam's voice boomed about their ears.

Kim got to her feet and nodded her head mutely.

"I *know* what you're up to," Miriam said threateningly. "You're not getting my secret, so stop spying on me and forget it. *Understand*?"

Elliot and Kim stood rooted to the spot in fear and nodded mechanically.

"Good!" said Miriam as she turned on her heels and went back to join Tiffany.

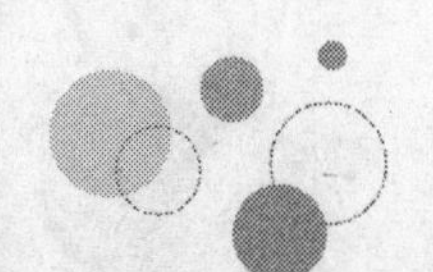



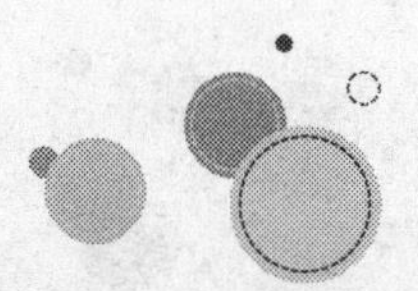

"Wow, Miriam, you can be really scary," said Tiffany uncomfortably.

"It's a *pageant*, Tiffany, you can't take prisoners," she replied matter-of-factly.

Up in the office Rikki, Emma and Cleo had seen the whole thing! Miriam waving her arms angrily in the air while Elliot and Kim cowered in fright as Tiffany, in shock, had looked on from a distance.

"She is *so* mean!" said Cleo horrified, forgetting that 20 minutes earlier she'd said she'd wanted to maim her meddlesome little sister.

"Ha! Yeah, she is, but look at that," said Rikki, pointing. "Miriam's outburst doesn't seem to have put Kim and Elliot off the scent!"

The three girls craned their necks in time to see Kim and Elliot as they ducked behind a buoy and then scampered along in pursuit of Miriam and Tiffany. They weren't giving up the chase that easily!

Secretly, Emma was proud of Elliot for

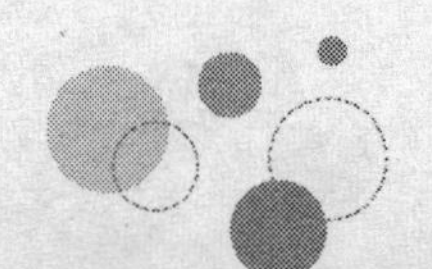

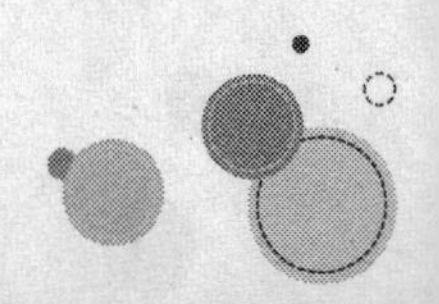

standing up to a bully, but now probably wasn't the time to mention that to the others!

"If we're going to make this work, we've got to make it look like Miriam's the one with all the powers," she said.

"Like how?" asked Cleo.

Emma grinned at Rikki.

"Ready?" she asked.

"Please, allow me," Rikki laughed, as she took a theatrical bow.

Below them, Miriam and Tiffany picked their way around the nets and ropes left on the marina to dry.

"This has *got* to be a safety hazard!" said Miriam, disgustedly. "Someone could slip over in all this water and break their leg."

Rikki stared out of the window at Miriam's and Tiffany's retreating backs and concentrated. She thought of hot showers and spa pools and rock pools warmed by the sun.

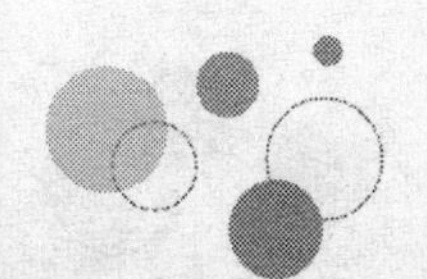



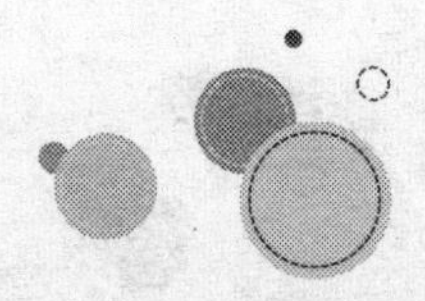

With a small flick of Rikki's hand, slowly the water on the marina began to evaporate! The steam billowed up from the planks and created a thick white cloud. And when it had cleared, Tiffany and Miriam were gone!

From their hiding place, Kim and Elliot gasped. It looked to them as if the two girls had disappeared in a puff of smoke!

"*Now* do you believe me?" hissed Kim.

Elliot, lost for words, nodded his head.

Two hours later, Kim and Elliot sat in the now-empty arena at the marine park.

Both of them had had to go home for lunch but they'd arranged to meet up afterwards to devise a plan. Miriam had to be stopped and they were the only ones who could do it!

"Tomorrow Miriam and my freak sister are both going to be at the Miss Sea Queen Pageant here at the marine park," said Kim, briefing Elliot like she'd seen it done on television police dramas. "This'll be a perfect time to expose them. We'll bring down the

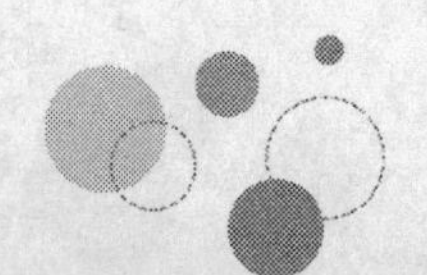



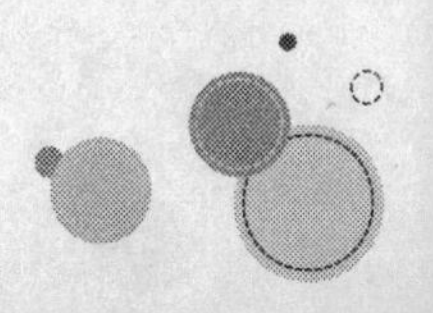

leader and the rest will follow."

Elliot shuffled from foot to foot as he thought of the magic they'd seen Miriam perform that morning.

"I'm scared," he said, embarrassed to admit it.

"That's exactly what they want, Elliot," said Kim matter-of-factly, as she unfolded the tourist map she'd picked up at the marine park entrance on the way in.

"Now listen carefully. You'll be here, next to this firehouse backstage." Kim stabbed at the map with her stumpy finger. "I'll be *here*, directly behind the stage. On my signal, you'll turn on the fire hydrant and angle it over this wall. The water will hit the stage, turning Miriam and Cleo into mermaids. And *us*... into heroes!"

It was a simple plan, but a very effective one.

"Any questions?" she asked as she expertly refolded the map.

"No," Elliot replied, his voice quavering in fear.

Kim put her hands on his shoulders and

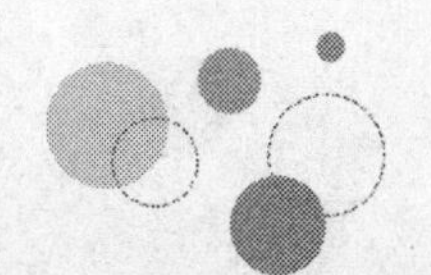



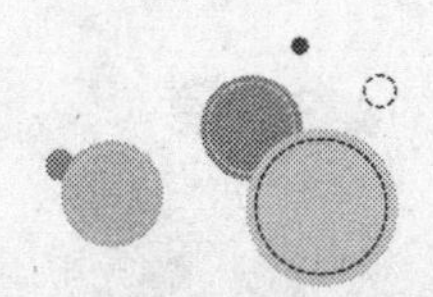

shook him slightly, all the while looking earnestly into his face.

"You *have* to be brave, Elliot," she said encouragingly.

"*I know, I know*," he replied irritably, wriggling out of her grasp.

But Kim wasn't really paying that much attention to Elliot and how he felt about the plan. Her mind had already raced ahead to the future. A future where she was Mermaid-Slayer Extraordinaire!

"Remember," she said, more to herself than Elliot. "The only ones with anything to fear… *are the mermaids*."

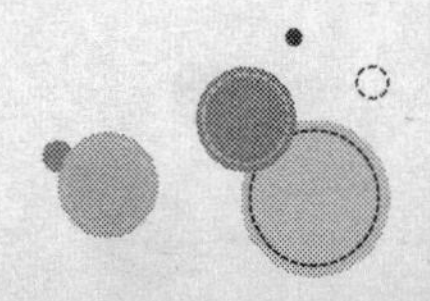

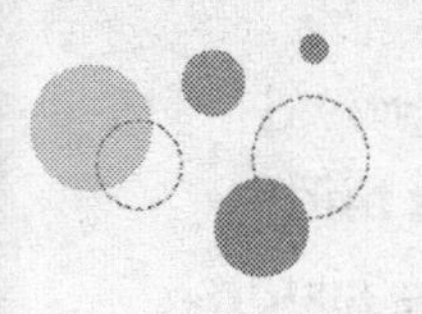

# Chapter 9

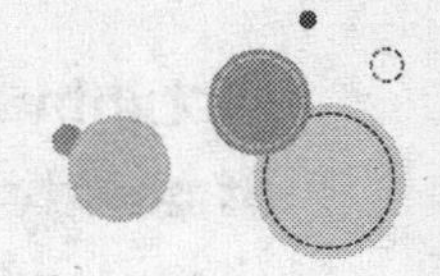

At 2.30 p.m. the next day, the Miss Sea Queen Pageant was already half over and Rikki was thankful about that! She had already finished a whole jumbo bucket of popcorn on her own, because of course Emma hadn't wanted any, and was starting to feel a bit queasy. Although that probably had more to do with the actual pageant than the amount of butter she'd asked the guy at the counter to heap onto the popcorn!

*These costumes are ridiculous! What has Tiffany come as? Is she meant to be a Greek goddess or an Academy Award statue? And this starfish* thing *hobbling on stage now!* Rikki snickered as Emma shot her a warning glance to shut her up.

On stage Mrs Geddes was excitedly introducing the next contestant.

"Next up we have Libby McIntyre as a… starfish!"

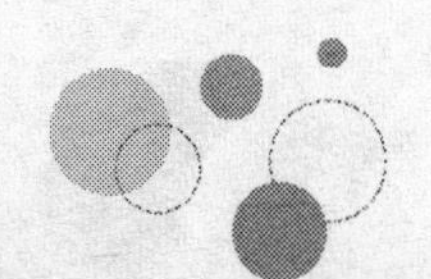



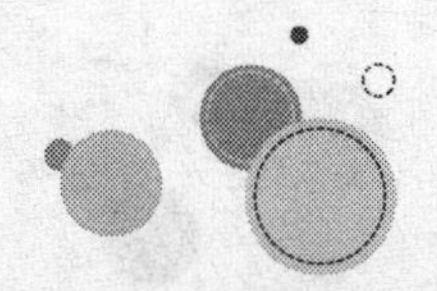

Libby stumbled out in front of the crowd of mostly mums and dads and brothers and sisters, who had come to see their older sisters competing for the title of Miss Sea Queen. Her costume was so stiff she found it hard to walk and the stage curtain had snagged on her barnacles. A ripple of laughter could be heard from pockets of the audience.

"This reminds me of a beautiful costume that *I* made..." Mrs Geddes gushed with admiration as Libby edged slowly forwards.

Rikki thought it looked more like a giant version of the purple spangly pot-scrubber she used when she did the washing up at home, but then she also had to admit to herself that she didn't know anything about sewing or dressing up; and after this display, she didn't want to!

"Who *are* these people?" Rikki asked Emma, with a look of horror on her face.

Emma, who had been applauding Libby McIntyre's costume, turned her cool appraising glance on Rikki.

"Rikki, at least *pretend* you're having fun," she scolded.

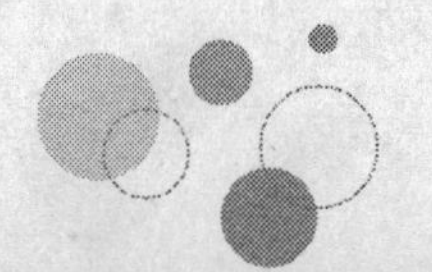



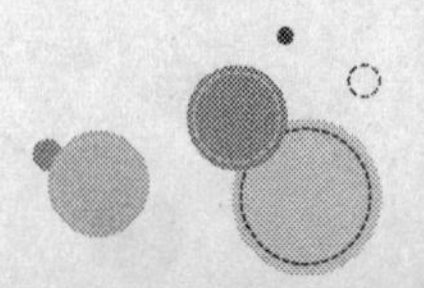

"But I'm *not*," Rikki replied sulkily, screwing up her face.

Emma ignored her. Sometimes Rikki could be so immature and rude!

"... and what a beautiful starfish she is," finished Mrs Geddes as Libby McIntyre's proud dad, who was sitting in the front row, took his seventh photograph for the family album.

The Miss Sea Queen Pageant stage had been set up in the far corner of the marine park, near the dodgem cars and roller-coaster, well away from the main display pools where the dolphins performed.

Elliot and Kim had climbed over a fence with a big 'Restricted Area' sign on it and weaved their way quietly past the ride operators having their break in the tents dotted around the grounds.

Now they found themselves in a deserted alleyway behind the Miss Sea Queen stage.

From where they stood, Elliot could see the kids on the roller-coaster as they whooshed

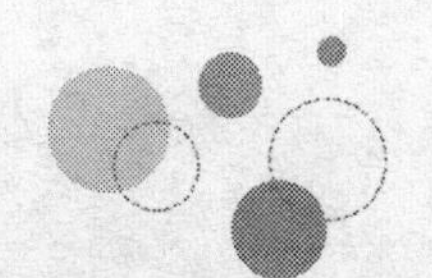



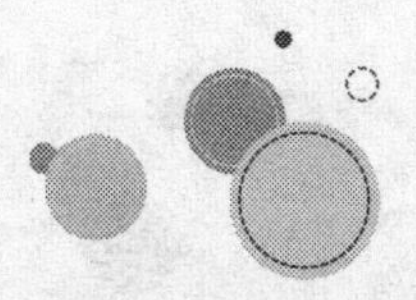

high up into the air before plummeting down again screaming. He wondered if any of them felt as sick as he did! All he knew for sure was that he was more frightened of what Kim would do if he chickened out now than if they were caught by the marine park security guys!

Kim had found the fire reel, which was on a wall to the right of the back of the stage and she mimed to Elliot that he was to stay there and wait for her signal.

"On my mark," she whispered to Elliot as he began to unwind the hose.

In the semi-darkness of the backstage area, Cleo waited excitedly, tugging her costume into shape and adjusting the giant headdress. Her mind wandered back to the events of the day before and how she had so narrowly avoided turning into a mermaid in front of Kim and her mum! She remembered how, as she lay helplessly on the floor with her tail slapping forlornly on the bathroom's tiles, she'd heard her mum tell Kim off for spying on her and this afternoon, when they were leaving to come to

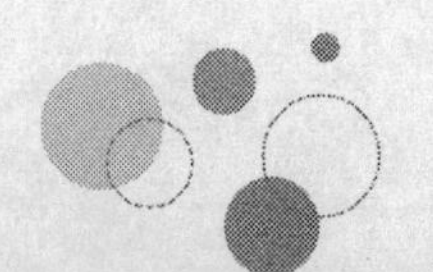



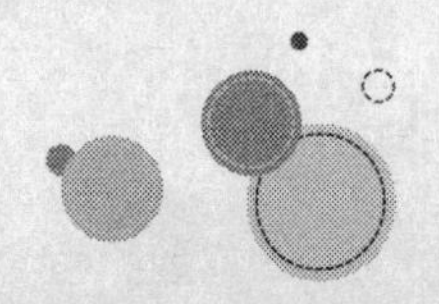

the pageant, Kim had said she hadn't wanted to come with them. Cleo just hoped Kim wasn't planning to do anything stupid.

She frowned slightly as she thought of all the naughty situations Kim had got mixed up in, in the last few years… but then some of them *had* been hilarious! Like the time Kim had wanted to be a great detective and had 'fingerprinted' their dog Boris and their cat Lucy. Of course, once they'd escaped from Kim's room, they'd left inky black paw prints all through the entire house! Their dad had been *really* angry, but Mum had gone straight into the bedroom and laughed her head off!

Cleo smiled brightly as she remembered her mum patiently showing her how to use the sewing machine so that she could work on the costume until late in the night, perfecting her tentacles and painting and gluing sequins all over her stockings.

Now here she was waiting for her name to be called next! She jiggled from foot to foot with nerves and hoped that her costume would be the winner. In fact, Cleo was so busy

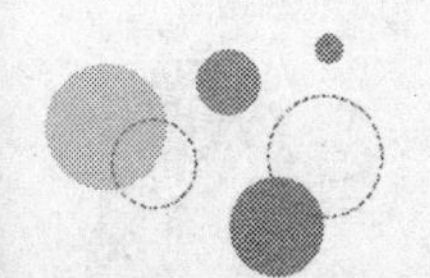



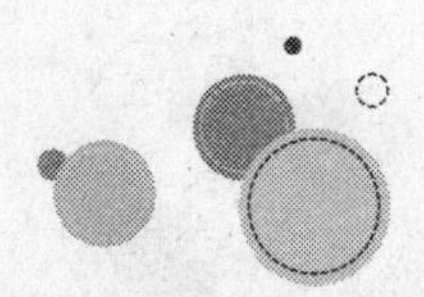

imagining what Miriam would do when she, Cleo, was presented with the winner's tiara, that she didn't notice first a nose and then the rest of a head poke out from behind the backstage curtain and look around quizzically.

But Kim had seen Cleo and quickly pulled her head back to safety behind the drapery. Kim's heart banged in her chest and she realized she felt almost as nervous as Elliot had looked when she left him at the fire reel!

Suddenly, from the front of the stage, Mrs Geddes announced, "Our next jewel of the sea is… Cleo Sertori!"

Cleo took a deep breath, gathered her tentacles around her, confidently parted the curtains and walked out onto the stage into the bright afternoon sun.

Although the crowd clapped politely, Mrs Geddes immediately sensed that something was wrong and turned to Cleo, her expression changing from affable pageant hostess to one of blank confusion.

Rikki and Emma, who had stood up out of their seats for a better view of Cleo's entrance,

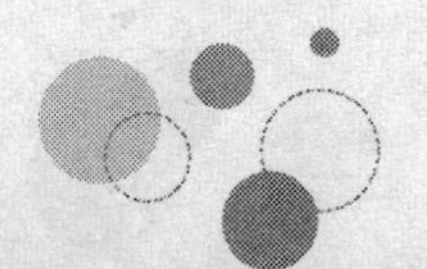



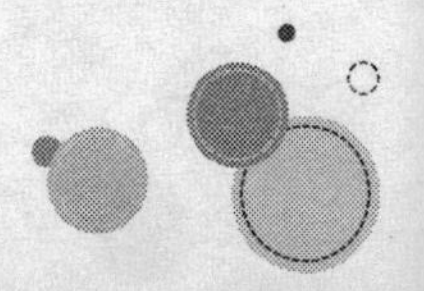

looked at each other questioningly.

As the subdued applause was quickly replaced by utter silence, it suddenly became very clear that not one person in the audience, including Cleo's mother, could work out exactly what sea creature Cleo was supposed to be!

*She looks like a wet sponge with sequins!* thought Rikki, careful not to snicker out loud.

Emma simply looked embarrassed and said nothing. Cleo was her best friend in the world, but she didn't always totally think things through before she did them. Why did she want to enter a Miss Sea Queen Pageant anyway?

On the other side of the seating bank, Cleo's parents looked equally confused.

"What *is* it?" Cleo's dad asked his wife. But all Cleo's mum could do was shrug her shoulders.

*She must've got the paint out*, Cleo's mum thought gloomily, *because it looked alright when I went to bed!*

And now it looked like a right mess!

The headdress she wore made Cleo look like

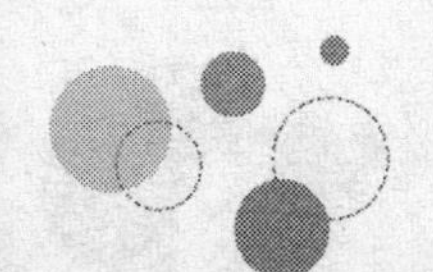



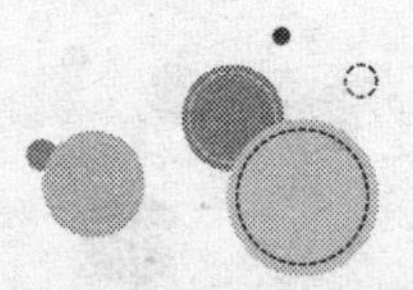

she had a massive purple mushroom growing out of her head! And her tentacles, which hung down from all sides of the headdress, were all stuck together because the glue Cleo had used to stick on her sequins hadn't quite dried properly.

On stage Mrs Geddes could sense possible disaster looming. It was her job as pageant hostess to compliment each contestant's costume, but how could she do that if she hadn't a clue what the costume was supposed to be! Plus, she didn't want to embarrass the girl who was so dedicated to her job at the marine park.

Mrs Geddes coughed nervously into the microphone and it squealed with feedback, drawing even more attention to the ever-increasing uncomfortable silence of the restless crowd.

"Um… ah… Cleo has chosen to come dressed as a…" Mrs Geddes turned to Cleo reluctantly, "Give us a hint?" she asked sweetly, all the while grinning until her jaw ached.

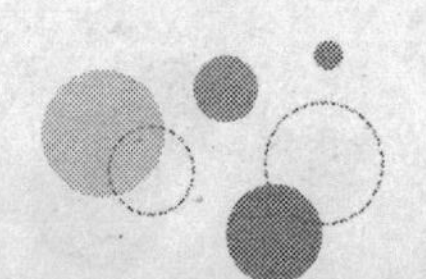

Cleo beamed widely at the audience. She had taken the hush of the crowd as a mark of appreciation for the work of art she called her costume!

"I'm a Portuguese Man o' War!" she announced triumphantly as she took a slight bow.

A sea of blank faces stared back at Cleo; still no one was any the wiser.

"It's a jellyfish!" cried Cleo, pleased that she'd kept the audience guessing.

*Honestly, I have* the *most original mind*, she thought dreamily to herself, *imagine what I could have come up with if I'd had more time!*

The audience *oohed* and *aahed* in appreciation. And because no one wanted to look stupid for not knowing what a Portuguese Man o' War was, Cleo's round of applause was easily the loudest and longest of the afternoon!

Rikki and Emma looked at each other with obvious relief in their eyes and jumped to their feet to show their support for their best friend.

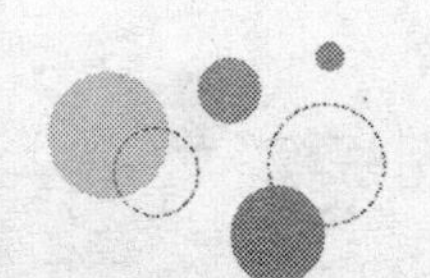



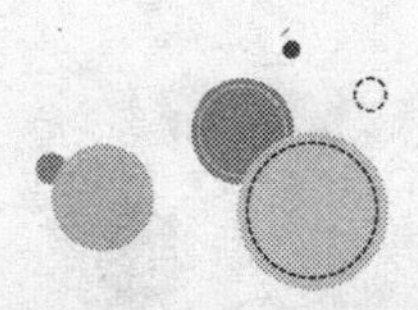

Kim sat behind the back curtain, listening to Cleo's applause.

*Oh, you won't be clapping when I expose my sister for the freak she is!* she thought nastily. *I'm going to uncover a whole coven of mer-weirdos and then we'll see who gets all the applause for being a heroine!*

She poked her nose through the gap in the curtain and caught sight of Miriam waiting to be called next, but in the semi-darkness of the backstage area, couldn't quite make out what her costume was meant to be.

Kim drew her knees up under her chin, hugged them to herself and smiled; everything was going according to her plan.

"Last, but by no means least, let's give a very warm welcome to Miriam Kent," said Mrs Geddes, more than happy to move on to the next contestant.

The curtains parted awkwardly as first a tail and then a silken torso appeared! It was Miriam dressed as a… mermaid!

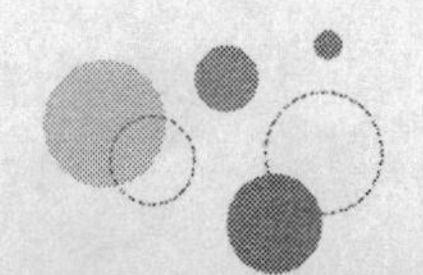



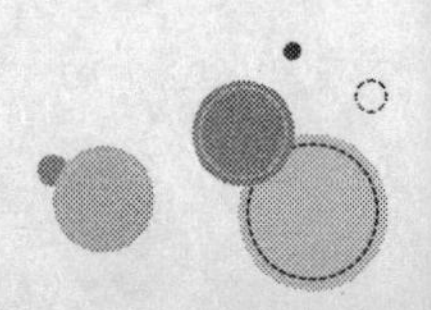

She had absolutely fallen in love with the idea of a mermaid costume and had spent so much time making and decorating it, but Miriam hadn't fully thought through how she was going to get on and off stage with a huge great tail! In the end a park employee had agreed to dress up as a lifesaver and wheel her around in one of the marine park's wheelchairs, which Tiffany and Miriam had hurriedly decorated just ten minutes before the pageant was due to begin.

"Oooooh, Miriam's a *mermaid*!" cried Mrs Geddes with a mixture of delight and relief on seeing a costume she could so easily recognize. And perhaps more importantly, one the audience could recognize!

In the audience, Emma took a deep breath and smiled broadly at Rikki.

*Miriam couldn't have played into our hands any better!* she thought happily.

If Kim was hanging around the pageant somewhere, and Emma was sure she was, then

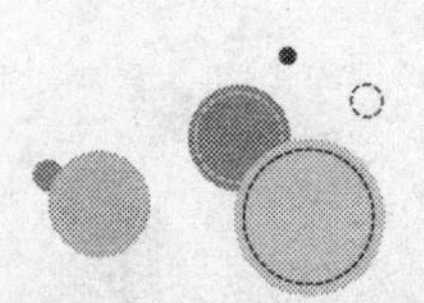

Miriam dressing up in a mermaid costume was perfect.

*Kim will take one look at Miriam, be totally convinced that she's a mermaid and stalk her until she finds out everything*, thought Emma, *and of course there will be* nothing *to find out!*

But Rikki was too busy emptying out the few crumbs left in the bottom of her popcorn tub to notice Emma's sudden change of mood.

"I might need this bucket to vomit in," she sneered in answer to Emma's questioning look.

On stage, Miriam smiled sweetly and waved to the crowd, many of whom were on their feet, clapping wildly.

But inside, Miriam was furious!

She had been so sure that Cleo was going to come dressed as a mermaid – she'd *seen* the website they'd been checking out at the Juice-Net Café!

*We were both meant to be dressed as mermaids and my costume was going to be so much better! But now she's come as… as… well,*

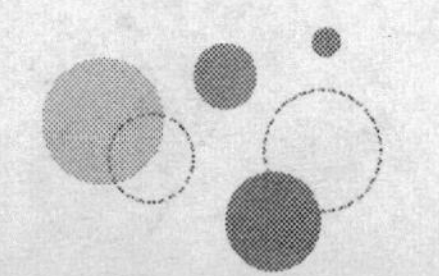



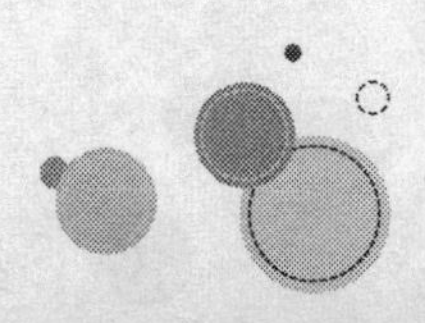

*whatever* that *is!* Miriam thought spitefully.

She had wanted to see Cleo humiliated! Instead Miriam was stuck in a poorly decorated wheelchair feeling like a beached whale!

"You were *supposed* to be a mermaid," Miriam hissed at Cleo, glaring at her with fury.

"No I wasn't," Cleo beamed back.

*Really? Where did she get that idea?* Thought Cleo innocently. *As if I'd go as a mermaid! That would really be asking for trouble.*

"Miriam, you look absolutely wonderful. Tell me, did you make this yourself?" asked Mrs Geddes, as she shoved the microphone into Miriam's face.

"All the sequins and beading are handmade," replied Miriam, shrugging her shoulders.

*Like she hadn't been up all night slaving over that cossie*, Rikki thought crossly.

"They're all handmade; isn't that wonderful!" Mrs Geddes cooed. "And that's all our contestants..."

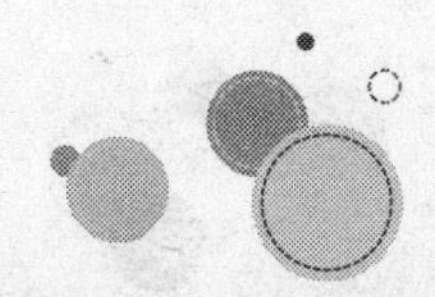

Backstage, Kim listened as the judges were introduced.

"There'll be a five minute break and then we'll be back to announce the winners!" she heard Mrs Geddes announce excitedly.

*It's now or never!* thought Kim happily. She couldn't wait to see what was going to happen when Elliot turned on that tap!

She jumped to the ground behind the stage and making sure no one was looking, darted over to the far corner of stage to double check that Elliot was still in position.

"Go Elliot, *now,*" she whispered as loud as she dared.

Elliot, his heart thumping with anticipation, heard the signal and immediately turned the tap on as hard as it would go, sending an arc of freezing water over the back of the stage.

He couldn't have positioned the nozzle better!

The water rained down on the stage in a soaking torrent and although he couldn't see anything from his position backstage, Elliot

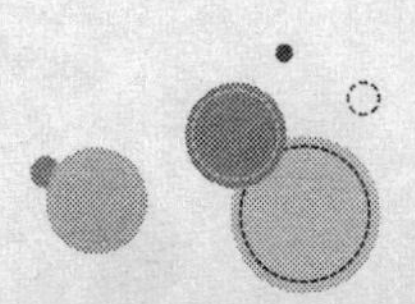

heard the squeals of shock echoing around the park…

On stage the pageant was in total chaos!

The contestants stared helplessly at each other as their costumes slowly fell apart under the power of the deluge. It was like someone from above was emptying buckets of icy water on their heads!

Three girls, their headdresses falling over their eyes, ran into each other and got all tangled up in the stage curtain.

Mrs Geddes, who couldn't decide whether she should run for shelter or try to calm everyone down, did nothing but stand on the spot and whimper softly.

Luckily Cleo had been on the far right of the stage and when the water had first arced over the curtain it had been Miriam who had taken the full force of the downpour. But Cleo knew that there was a very real danger that *she* could get wet if the angle of the water changed or the

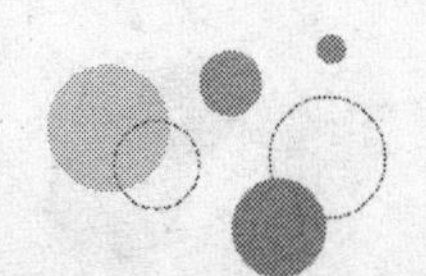



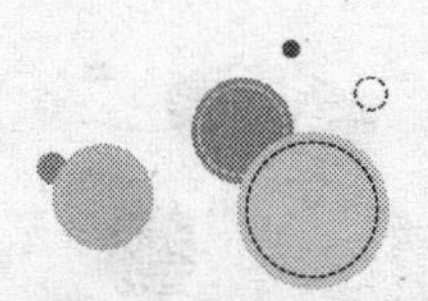

stage became flooded!

*I mustn't panic. I can control water and that's* all *I need to do*, she said to herself, and standing very still with her palms facing outwards, she concentrated as hard as she could. She remembered how many times she'd manipulated water in the past and *knew* she could do it now when it really mattered!

*Keep dry, keep dry, keep dry,* she repeated over and over again.

And as the water continued to splash down all around her, the drops seemed to bend and bounce and not one of them landed on Cleo.

She bit her lip and smiled as she watched the other contestants run helplessly around the stage.

Rikki and Emma had jumped to their feet the second they saw the first jet of water spurt over the curtain.

*Oh no, Cleo!* thought Emma desperately, as she craned her neck to see over the man in front of her. The whole audience was standing

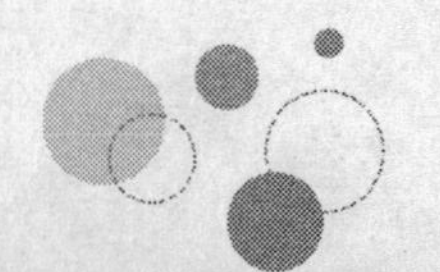

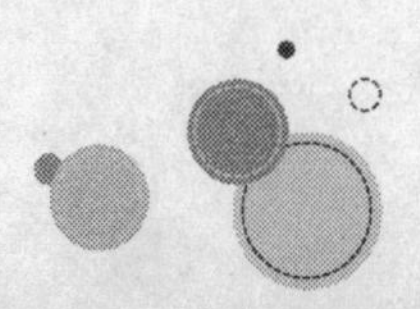

up and she couldn't see a thing. *What's going on? Where is that water coming from?*

Suddenly the crowd parted a little in front of her and she had a clear view to the stage.

And there stood Cleo, smiling serenely as she surveyed the pandemonium that had broken out around her.

Emma felt faint with relief – Cleo was totally dry!

Now that they knew that Cleo was safe, she could relax and enjoy the spectacle. Emma nudged Rikki and pointed through the crowd to where Cleo stood on stage.

*Maybe this hasn't been such a waste of an afternoon after all*, thought Rikki happily, as she watched the rivers of makeup run down the contestants' faces. And then she spotted Miriam…

"Look at the state of *her*," Rikki sniggered as she pointed out Miriam, her mascara smudged blackly around her eyes, to Emma. "She looks like a panda bear!" And to Rikki's surprise, Emma doubled up in hysterics.

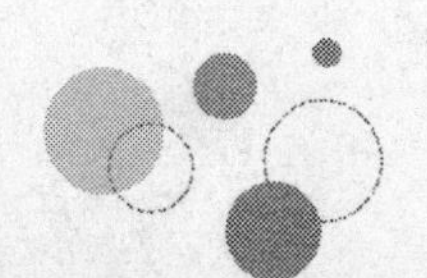



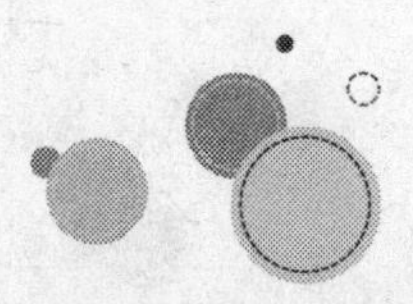

Kim stood behind the back curtain and listened to the shrieks coming from the stage.

*I'll be famous,* she thought proudly, *no one's going to forget what happened here today. I'll be known far and wide as the Mermaid Hunter!*

Suddenly she heard voices from back stage. It was a couple of marine park workers yelling at each other as they tried to find where the water was coming from.

Kim knew it wouldn't be long before they searched the rear of the stage and she didn't want to be around when they did. It was time to shut off the water and get to work on the second part of the plan: the unmasking!

Meanwhile Elliot had completely forgotten how frightened he'd been earlier and was having a great time!

He pointed the hose this way and that, laughing loudly at the different reactions he got. If he directed the hose over to stage right, he heard high-pitched screams and running; if he aimed the hose over to stage left, he heard a low moaning and the squeal of the microphone.

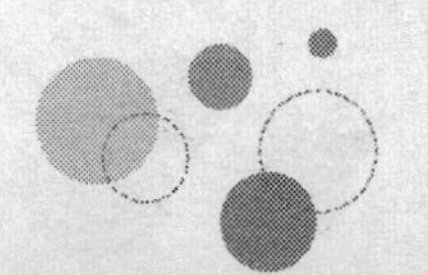



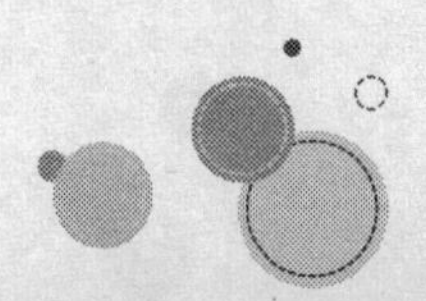

In fact, when Kim appeared and gave him the signal to cut the water, Elliot was a little disappointed!

Still grinning madly, Elliot dropped the hose and quickly shut off the tap, turning back just in time to see Kim part the backstage curtain and disappear inside.

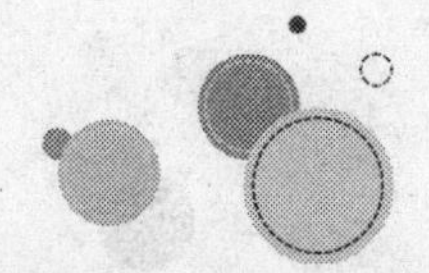

# Chapter 10

It would be hard to say who was more surprised when Kim rushed onto the stage!

Certainly Kim's parents looked at each other in shock.

*Surely this whole water thing can't have been Kim's doing*, Mrs Sertori said to herself, as she recalled Kim's recent strange behaviour.

Mrs Geddes marched over to Kim.

"What on earth do you think you're *doing*?! Who *are* you?" she asked angrily.
Kim ignored her and peered down at the expectant faces looking up at her from the crowd.

"I'm Kim," she said simply. "And I need that microphone," she added, making a grab for the mic still in Mrs Geddes's hand.

But Mrs Geddes wasn't about to give it to

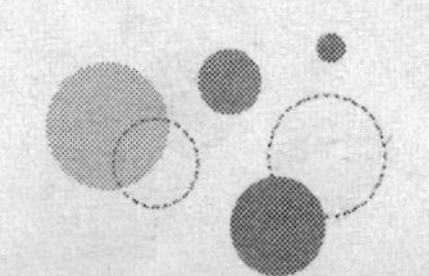



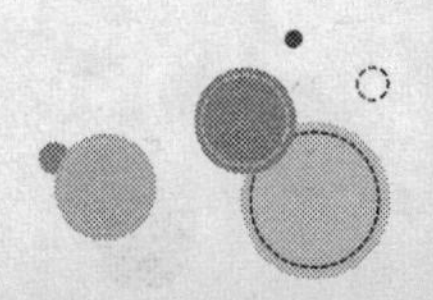

Kim that easily.

Kim pulled; Mrs Geddes scowled and pulled back.

But Kim was not only much younger, she was much *much* more determined and with a final tug, she yanked the microphone from Mrs Geddes's firm grasp and looked around the stage for her victim.

And there sat Miriam in all her mermaid finery.

"I knew it! There are mermaids on the Gold Coast!" Kim announced triumphantly, her voice ringing out over the audience.

"And *she*," Kim pointed dramatically at Miriam, "is their evil leader!"

Miriam rolled her eyes. *Really, this pipsqueak is too pathetic!*

"Somebody shut that dirty little moron up!" she growled, as she looked around for someone to help her as she struggled to get up. But Miriam's costume was so tight, she couldn't move! She was a prisoner in her chair!

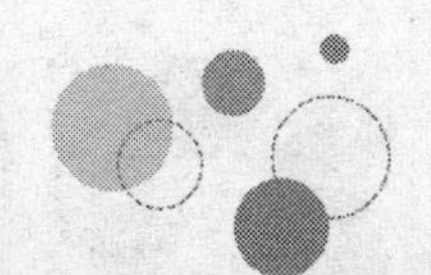



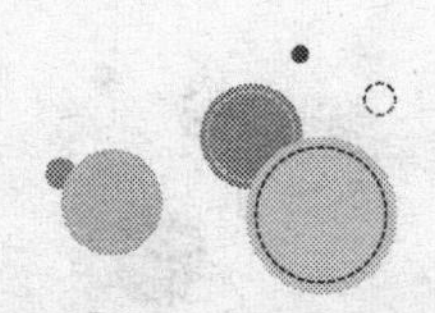

Cleo's parents looked at each other in shame and confusion as the audience began to titter with amusement.

Kim heard the laughter and her heart sank as she realized that no one believed her! She knew she'd have to produce some hard evidence; then they'd appreciate what a hero she was for exposing the mermaid threat!

"My sister is one too!" Kim added, her voice full of desperation, as she pointed out Cleo.

Cleo smiled sheepishly. She felt sorry for Kim as the crowd began to laugh even harder, but what could she do? Kim had brought it all on herself and now she was going to have to get herself out of it.

Suddenly from backstage, one of the marine park workers appeared holding a very guilty-looking Elliot by the arm.

"*She* made me do it!" Elliot yelled immediately, pointing to Kim.

The audience roared with laughter.

*It's like a really really bad pantomime*, thought Rikki with glee.

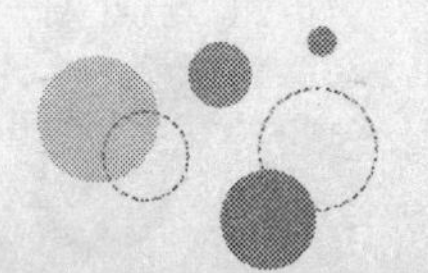



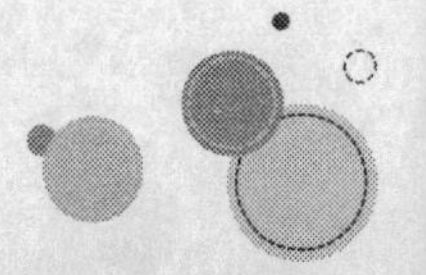

At least *she* didn't have an embarrassing brother or sister who would crash a beauty pageant and make fools of themselves.

She glanced out of the corner of her eye at Emma's reddening face, but Rikki couldn't tell if it was humiliation or anger that caused her face to flush. *Elliot is gonna get it!* thought Rikki and she was surprised to find that she felt bit sorry for him.

On stage, Kim waved her arms about wildly.

"They're evil and dangerous!" she screamed, but she saw that no one was listening; they were too busy falling about laughing!

Kim threw down the microphone, raced over to Miriam and bent over her tail.

"Look!" she yelled proudly to anyone who would listen, as she grabbed handfuls of tulle and silk and pulled at them with all her strength.

"Get away from me, you freak!" screamed Miriam, as she tried to twist her body away and out of Kim's grasp.

But Kim pulled some more, tearing the

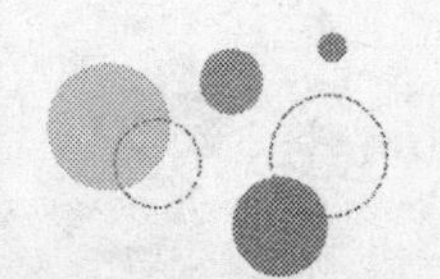



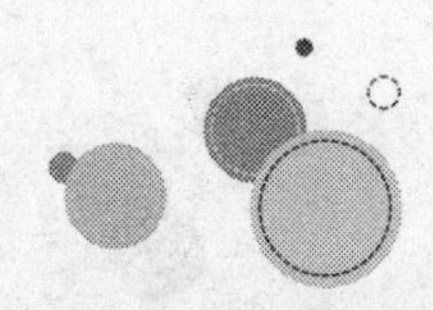

costume to shreds and uncovering Miriam's feet.

"Get away from me! *What are you doing*?" Miriam shrieked again, trying to aim a kick in Kim's direction.

Just as suddenly as she'd started, Kim suddenly stopped, her hands covered in sequins and baubles as she stared down at the torn fabric and Miriam's bare legs beneath it.

"Why is your tail tearing?" she asked, stunned.

"Because it's a *costume*, you weirdo!" Miriam snarled. "Just you *wait*…"

Now that her legs were half-free, Miriam pulled herself out of the chair and with some difficulty, heaved herself to her feet.

"I'm gonna *get* you!" She screeched as she jumped menacingly towards Kim.

From the side of the stage, Cleo could see from the expression on Kim's face that she was beginning to realize what a *big* mistake she'd made. *If only I hadn't written that stupid diary!* she thought guiltily.

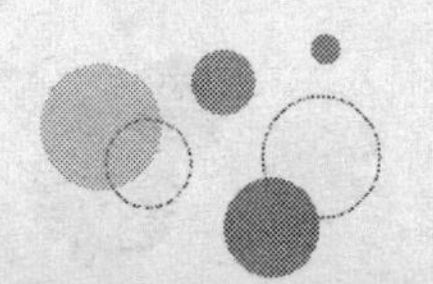



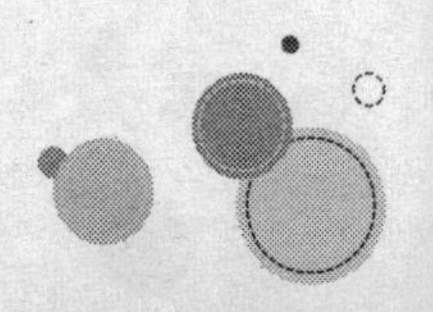

But Cleo could also see that even though Miriam's tattered costume allowed her some movement, it was still very tight around her knees and she watched fascinated as Miriam lost her balance, gave a startled cry and toppled off the stage!

In the audience, Rikki watched in amazement, laughing happily and hoping that one of the contestants' parents had videoed the pageant. *This is exactly the sort of thing that should be on 'Funniest Home Videos'!* Rikki thought, giggling to herself.

Miriam lay helpless on the ground, thrashing around in an effort to get up while people in the audience took photos of her with their mobile phones.

She'd never been so embarrassed in all her life!

"*Well,* any help here?" shouted Miriam crossly to Mrs Geddes and Tiffany as they watched gob-smacked from onstage.

Quickly, Tiffany leapt off stage to rescue her friend from the crowd of onlookers. But inside

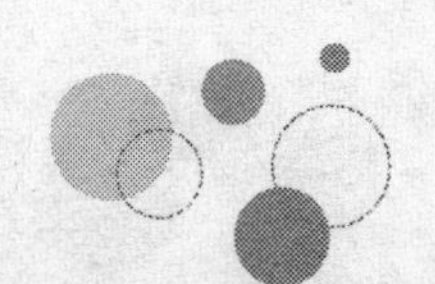



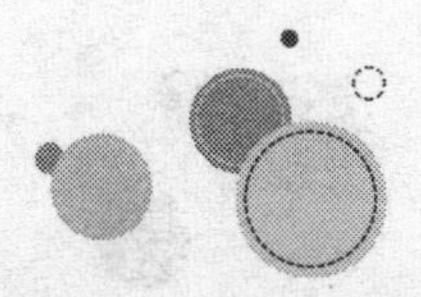

she couldn't help but wonder whether perhaps, just perhaps, Miriam deserved a bit of public humiliation. She'd been really mean to those two kids and now they'd got their own back…

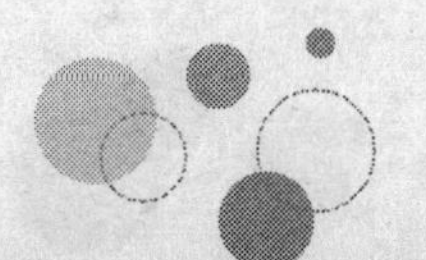



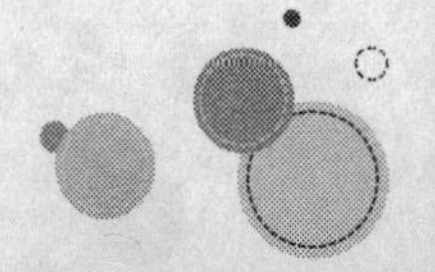

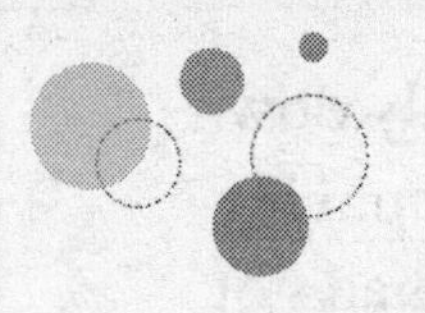

# Chapter 11

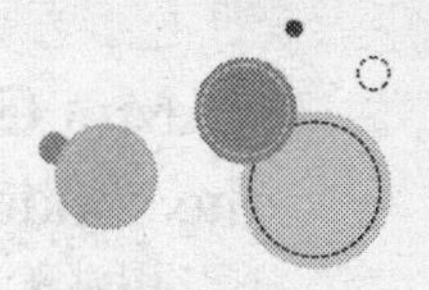

It was all over. Most of the contestants, wet and angry, had left half an hour earlier and now the few stragglers that had remained were packing up to go.

Miriam and Tiffany were among them.

"I'm *so* sorry, Miriam. I…" Tiffany began.

"You *should* be," Miriam butted in angrily. "You left me there on the ground. I felt like a complete idiot!"

Tiffany stared at the ground. *Miriam's right, I didn't react quick enough*, she thought sadly.

Both girls looked at each other and wondered if their friendship could survive such a terrible blow.

Suddenly, from the side of the stage, they heard Mrs Geddes call out.

"Tiffany? Tiffany *darling*?"

"Yes Mrs Geddes?" Tiffany called back enquiringly.

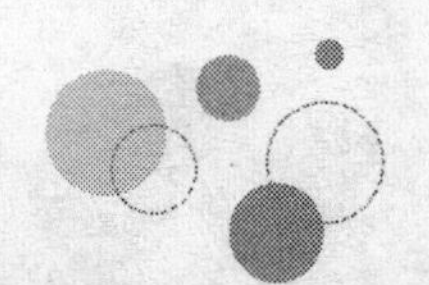



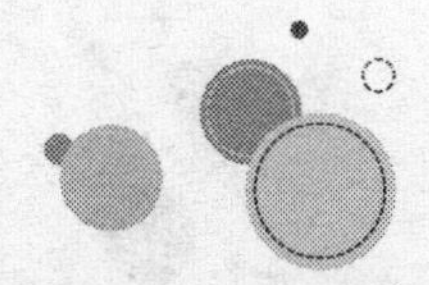

Mrs Geddes picked her way carefully down the sodden steps and came over to them. Her hair had dried out after the soaking it had got and it stuck out in every direction! She looked a very different person from the one that had stood so perfectly groomed on the stage two hours earlier.

"This is for you," she said as she placed the Miss Sea Queen tiara on Tiffany's head.

"*What*? *Me*? Oh *thank* you," said Tiffany with genuine excitement as she threw her arms around Mrs Geddes and gave her a big hug.

Miriam snorted and turning on her heels, stomped off without a word of congratulation for her friend.

Kim saw, from her hiding place under the stage, Mrs Geddes present Tiffany with the winner's tiara and gave a chuckle of satisfaction as she watched Miriam angrily march off.

Now that the coast was clear and she thought it was safe to come out from her hidey-hole, she squeezed herself out from under the stage and stood standing to look around for a

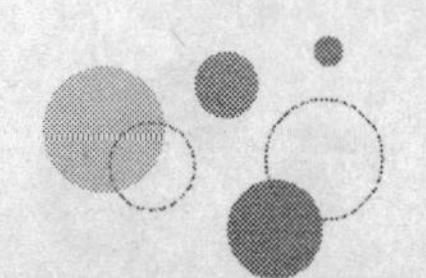



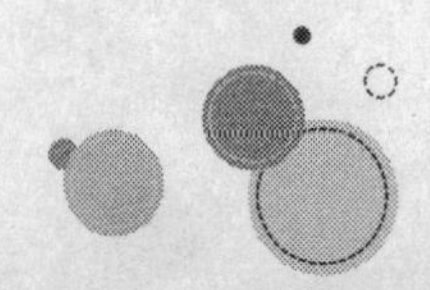

moment. Kim stretched and yawned loudly. It had been a long, tiring day! Her parents had grounded her for a month and Mrs Geddes had banned her from coming within 200 metres of another Miss Sea Queen Pageant, but Kim felt strangely happy; she *had* exposed Miriam, not as a mermaid perhaps, but as a selfish, mean human being.

*My work here is done*, she thought, smiling to herself.

"Kim?"

Kim jumped and spun around in fright. She hadn't heard Cleo's footsteps on the wet grass. "You *scared* me!" she exclaimed, putting her hand on her beating chest. "Don't *do* that."

"Sorry," Cleo smiled at her sister, before continuing. "Hey, Kim, I *know* you stole my diary. Is that where you got all those crazy ideas from?" Cleo asked, gesturing to the stage.

Kim folded her arms and stared up at her sister huffily.

"Dad says I'm not allowed to talk to anyone," she replied.

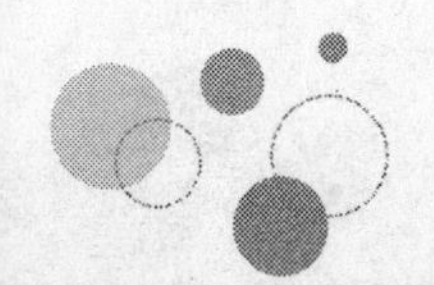



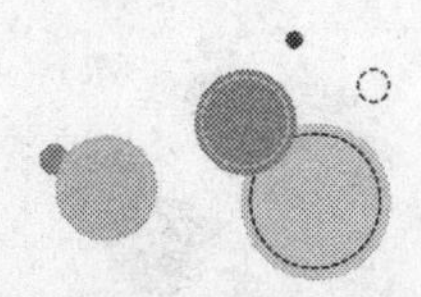

"Kim, that diary was an English assignment. We had to rewrite fairytales and I chose the Little Mermaid. It's fiction," Cleo said reasonably, hoping that Kim would believe her!

"But what about your tail? You had one at home." Kim's eyes narrowed thoughtfully. "I *saw* it."

Cleo felt physically sick.

"Aaaaaah, that was my first attempt at a costume," said Cleo, thinking quickly. "But I couldn't wear it because it shrunk."

Kim stared at Cleo for a minute.

"And the fish tank?" Kim said, trying to catch Cleo out in a lie.

"Like I told you, the fish were in the bucket," replied Cleo warily.

Kim looked her sister up and down and exhaled deeply.

"I'm *such* an idiot! As if *you* could be a mermaid, you can't even swim!" said Kim rudely.

Cleo smiled. "You're right," she said.

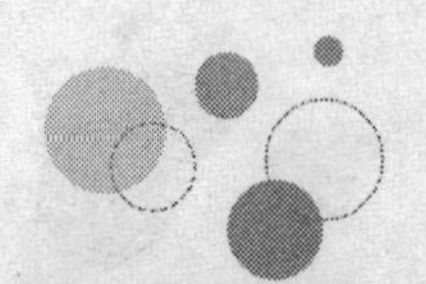

# Chapter 12

The three girls looked at Lewis expectantly. He'd asked them to meet him in the cave on Mako Island in order to tell them what his scientific tests had uncovered.

But Lewis, being Lewis, was taking his time about it!

"Well?" said Ricki impatiently, her tail slapping lightly in the water of the moon pool.

Lewis took a sip of his drink and pushed the inner tyre tube he was floating in a little farther away from the side of the pool.

"The story is I've tested everything; the water, the rocks, the soil, the lichen even the dust," he said mysteriously.

"And what did you find?" asked Emma eagerly.

"Everything's normal," Lewis shrugged, causing the rubber tube to rock unsteadily in the water.

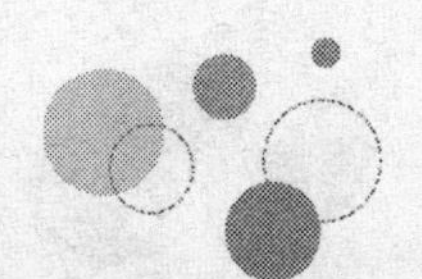



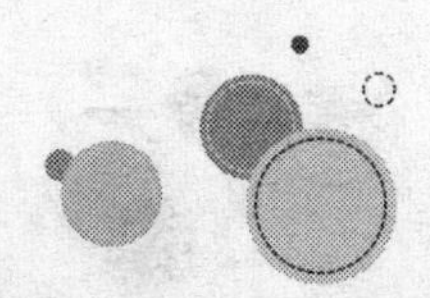

"So that's *it*? You're done?" asked Emma, sounding disappointed.

"Hey, I *am* putting in one hundred percent," replied Lewis, flicking water at Emma.

Rikki rolled her eyes. *Typical!* she thought to herself. *We're never going to get to the bottom of this!*

Aloud she said, "So Cleo, what did you do with the diary?"

"Don't worry, I took care of it," Cleo replied with a mischievous smile. "No one's going to find it *ever* again."

A long way out to sea, a school of dolphins frolicked in the cool water; rising to the surface before spinning down to the depths of sea floor where Cleo's diary lay, its pages waving like the tentacles of a sea anemone in the swirling currents.

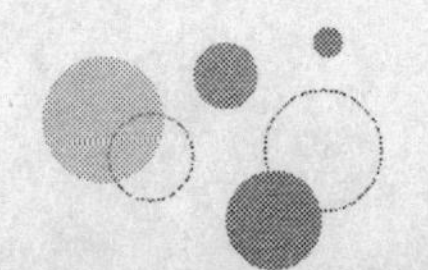



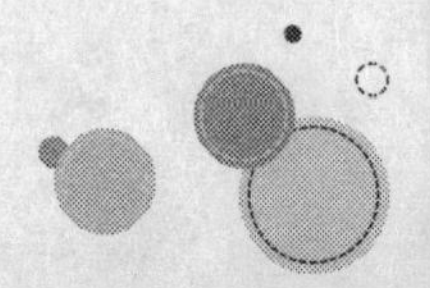